TALES FROM BEYOND THE BRAIN

TALES FROM BEYOND THE BRAIN

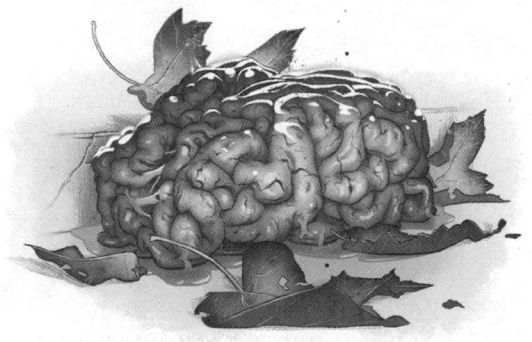

JEFF SZPIRGLAS

ILLUSTRATED BY
STEVEN P. HUGHES

ORCA BOOK PUBLISHERS

Library and Archives Canada Cataloguing in Publication

Title: Tales from beyond the brain / Jeff Szpirglas; illustrated by Steven P. Hughes.
Names: Szpirglas, Jeff, author. I Hughes, Steven P., 1989– illustrator.

Description: Short stories.

Identifiers: Canadiana (print) 20190065575 I Canadiana (ebook) 20190065605 I
ISBN 9781459820791 (softcover) I ISBN 9781459820807 (PDF) I
ISBN 9781459820814 (EPUB)

Classification: LCC PS8637.Z65 T35 2019 I DDC jC813/.6—dc23

Library of Congress Control Number: 2019934051
Simultaneously published in Canada and the United States in 2019

Summary: A collection of stories for middle readers that
ranges from the hilarious to the horrifying.

*Orca Book Publishers is committed to reducing the consumption of nonrenewable resources in the
making of our books. We make every effort to use materials that support a sustainable future.*

Orca Book Publishers gratefully acknowledges the support for its publishing programs provided
by the following agencies: the Government of Canada, the Canada Council for the Arts and the
Province of British Columbia through the BC Arts Council and the Book Publishing Tax Credit.

Edited by Tanya Trafford
Design by Jenn Playford
Illustrations and cover image by Steven P. Hughes
Author photo by Danielle Saint-Onge

ORCA BOOK PUBLISHERS
orcabook.com

Printed and bound in Canada.
22 21 20 19 • 4 3 2 1

A few of these stories have appeared elsewhere in different forms. "Scratch" was previously published in 2013 in *Dark
Moon Digest* (Young Adult Edition, Issue 1); "Chewy Ones" was previously published in 2011 in *31 Days of Halloween*;
"Evil Eye" was adapted into a full-length novel of the same name and published by Star Crossed Press in 2012.

FOR DANIELLE, LÉO, RUBY, ALWAYS.

CONTENTS

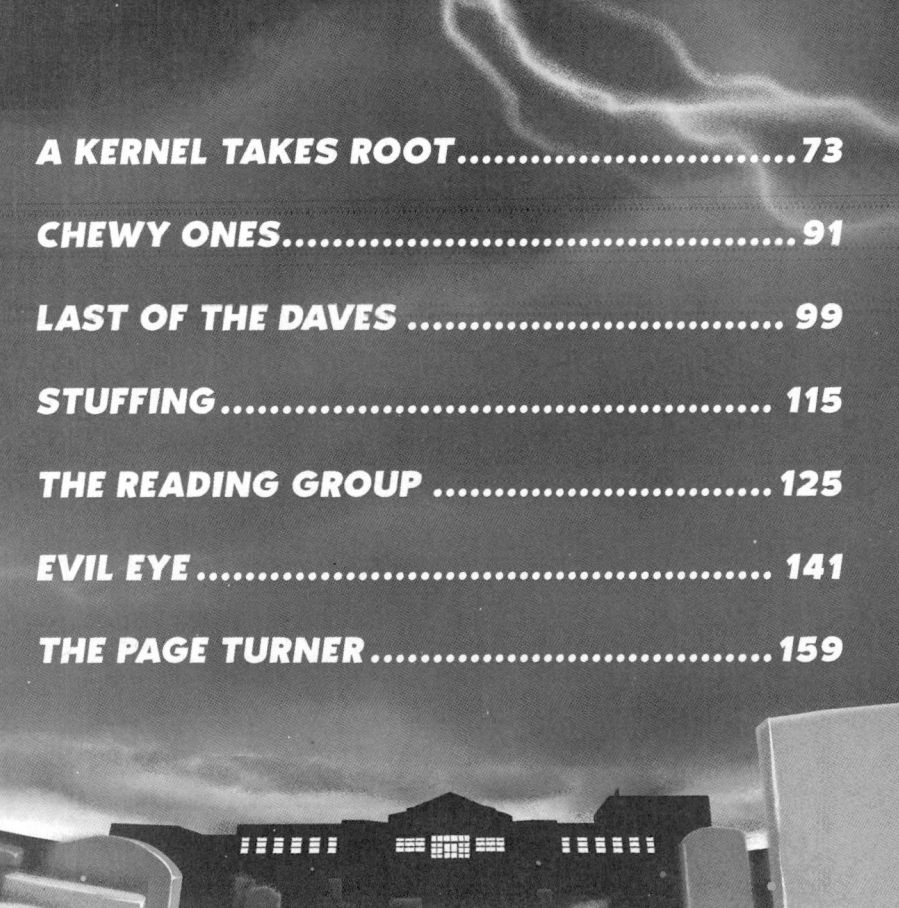

AN APPLE A DAY

Megan knew that the Student of the Day was expected to give Mr. Oakwood an apple. It was one of those things nobody questioned, like standing up to sing the national anthem, or lining up with your class outside the school when the entry bell rang.

The Student of the Day was Mr. Oakwood's way of giving each kid in the class all of the jobs to do—running the attendance, handing out materials, helping to tidy the class library. But the apple payment? Mr. Oakwood never asked for them. You just placed one at the corner of his desk when you gathered the work folders to hand out. No school day truly began without the loud crunch of Mr. Oakwood chowing down on his daily apple before morning announcements.

Megan sat close enough to Mr. Oakwood's desk to see every manner of apple find its way there: Red, Golden Delicious, Spartan, Northern Spy, Granny Smith. There had probably been more kinds of apples placed on Mr. Oakwood's desk than there were kids in the class.

One Thursday morning Megan watched Lewis Stoller mope into class with his head hung down, his hands jammed deep into his pockets. When he looked up, Megan noticed his eyes were red and puffy.

Lewis stopped at the corner of Mr. Oakwood's desk. There were heaps of books and binders and file folders jammed with all sorts of papers, including drawings the teacher had torn from the hands of distracted students. The desk was messier than the aftermath of a Category 5 hurricane...except for a single perfectly clear spot in the corner reserved for Oakwood's Apple.

Lewis stared at the empty space. He shifted his weight from foot to foot and then turned his head to glance at the blackboard in the distance. His name was scrawled in chalk letters below the sign that said **STUDENT OF THE DAY.**

Lewis sniffed and reached into his pocket. Slowly he pulled out a small red lump. His hand was shaking so violently that it took Megan a second to figure out what she was seeing. It was an apple so tiny and bruised you'd be hard pressed to call the thing edible.

Breathing heavily, Lewis placed the apple on the desk corner and backed away. He turned around only to bump right into Mr. Oakwood's bulky frame.

Using his finger and thumb like a pair of tweezers, Mr. Oakwood reached over Lewis and lifted the apple to eye level. He inspected every blemish and bruise as if poring over the flaws in a diamond. His eyes narrowed, and he shifted his focus from the apple to Lewis. Normally, Mr. Oakwood would give the apple an approving crunch. This time he deposited it into his sweater pocket with a scowl.

Megan was good at noticing things. Like how many extra jobs Mr. Oakwood had for Lewis that day. Lewis had to stay in during recess to tidy his own desk. He had to reorganize all the dusty old books in the class library alphabetically. And wash the blackboard too. Megan sat close enough to Lewis to see that when their English assignments were handed back, his had THIS IS NO GOOD. TRY AGAIN. scrawled across the top in red block letters.

Suddenly Lewis was crying.

No, sobbing.

He crumpled up his work and tossed it on the floor.

"Is something the matter, Lewis?" Mr. Oakwood asked.

Lewis stormed out of the room and into the hall.

Megan saw a satisfied grin slide across Mr. Oakwood's face. She peered over her desk and stared at the paper on the floor. She could read the title of Lewis's story, "Why I Love My Family."

After the lunch bell rang, Mr. Oakwood began to sort the papers that had collected on his desk into neat little piles. Usually the Student of the Day did that, but Lewis had been sent to the office for leaving the classroom without permission.

While the rest of her classmates ate their lunches, Megan got out of her seat and approached the teacher.

"It's about the apple, isn't it?" she asked quietly.

"I beg your pardon?" Mr. Oakwood put his hands into his sweater pockets and pulled the material down low, stretching it across his thick frame.

"Lewis didn't give you a good apple, so you made him stay in for recess—"

"He's the Student of the Day, and I need help," Mr. Oakwood replied.

"You didn't like the apple he gave you."

"Lewis Stoller gave me a *bad* apple."

"And you need your apples to be perfect, don't you?"

Megan heard a muffled crunch. She didn't need Mr. Oakwood to pull his hands out of his pockets to know he had just squeezed the tiny apple into a pulp.

Megan decided she should probably stop talking. As she turned to head back to her desk, a flutter of movement caught her eyes. Something small buzzed past the windowsill.

Mr. Oakwood's eyes bulged in their sockets. "A bee!" he exclaimed. "Quick, kill the thing!"

The teacher leaped onto his chair as the flying insect loop-de-looped around the room.

The bee landed on the edge of Mr. Oakwood's desk. Megan stepped closer to inspect it. "*Anthophora*," she mused, grabbing a piece of paper off the desk. She gently placed it beside the bee. The bee crawled up onto the paper.

"You're crazy!" someone said in a squeaky voice. Megan thought it was one of the other kids in the room but then realized it was Mr. Oakwood.

Megan shook her head. "You don't want to move, Mr. Oakwood. Or even scream. That will only make it angry."

Carefully balancing the paper, Megan walked past the teacher and a cluster of terrified kids. She opened the window and shook the paper until the bee flew away. Then she turned back to face the class. "It's just a bee. Nothing to worry about, as long as you keep calm."

"You're weird," Megan heard one of her classmates mutter.

Megan shrugged. People had been saying things like that about her since she was a little girl. She wasn't afraid of anything creepy-crawly. Megan figured it was because she was kind of like a bee herself. People kept their distance, and that suited her just fine.

But, like a bee, when Megan got angry, she could sting.

And Megan was very, *very* angry with Mr. Oakwood.

On Monday morning Megan's heart thumped heavily in her chest as she approached Mr. Oakwood's desk. As usual, amid the chaos of papers and files, a small corner of the desk had been cleared for her offering.

Megan dug her hands into her pockets. In her left pocket she could feel the round globe of the apple her mother had given her. She squeezed its spherical form between the pads of her fingertips and the palm of her hand. The fruit resisted her touch. She tapped it with a fingernail. The apple was ripe but firm, just the way Mr. Oakwood liked it. There was not a bump or scratch on it. Megan wondered how long her mother had scoured the grocery store, looking for the perfect one. A few minutes? A few hours?

Megan pulled her hand out of her other pocket and placed the fig on Mr. Oakwood's desk.

A shadow appeared to sail past her. She felt a gust of wind. Papers fluttered. When she looked up, Mr. Oakwood was standing before her, eyeing the strange object on his desk.

"Hello, Megan. What's this?"

He had broken his own rule, Megan noted. Mr. Oakwood never discussed his payment.

Maybe that was because nobody ever forgot to bring him an apple. Even if it was mealy and pitiful.

"It's a fig," Megan said.

Mr. Oakwood picked it up and studied it. "A *fig*?"

"I know you like apples, but we didn't have any at home. Figs are tasty too."

"Oh." Mr. Oakwood looked disappointed. Megan had *always* brought him an apple when she was Student of the Day. But there was something else in his expression too. Curiosity.

Megan's father had taught her all about being curious. He worked with insects for the museum. He was an entomologist, and his job was studying tiny creatures. He was excellent at spotting little details, like how the antennae on one species of ant were bent on a slightly different angle than those of another species. He could count the spots on a ladybug and tell you if it came from North Carolina or Southern California. Megan's dad spent most of his time peering at the world through magnifying glasses. From him Megan had learned to spot little details too, like the expression on Mr. Oakwood's face.

He wanted to eat the fig. Megan knew this at once. As she turned to go back to her desk, she recognized the sound of chewing behind her. The fig wasn't crunchy like an apple, but it was tasty.

She heard Mr. Oakwood swallow, and she smiled.

Megan didn't mind when Mr. Oakwood dropped a stack of science textbooks on her desk in the middle of silent reading, even though the sudden noise made her gasp and drop her own book. She didn't mind when Mr. Oakwood glowered at her and ordered her to stay in during morning recess and erase all the penciled-in graffiti in them.

All the while, she kept her eye on Mr. Oakwood, watching and waiting.

The end-of-recess bell rang. In a few moments the hallway was buzzing with hundreds of kids, throwing their jackets onto hooks and changing from outdoor shoes into indoor shoes. Twenty or so spilled in through the door and shuffled back to their seats.

As Megan finished putting the books away, Mr. Oakwood told the kids to assemble at the front of the room for a math lesson. He'd only started to write a few math questions on the blackboard when he clutched his stomach and pitched forward.

Matthew Reyes, one of Megan's classmates, raised an eyebrow. "Are you feeling okay, Mr. Oakwood?"

Mr. Oakwood swallowed. Hard. He had a far-off look in his eyes, the kind you get when you suddenly want to throw up. "I'm fine."

Megan knew Mr. Oakwood was not fine. She could see little beads of sweat popping up on his forehead.

"Maybe it was something you ate," Lewis said.

"I said I'm fine."

"You did eat Megan's weird fruit," Lewis said.

"It wasn't an apple," Matthew added. He hadn't raised his hand, but Mr. Oakwood was too busy wiping the sweat from his brow and trying not to puke to notice that kids were speaking out of turn.

"It was a fig!" another student chimed in. "I've eaten figs before."

Megan decided it was time to explain. "It's a caducous fig," she said. "Mr. Oakwood, did you know that figs are pollinated by wasps?"

Mr. Oakwood blinked once, twice. He held his hands in front of his eyes and waved his fingers. "Huh?"

"It's true," she say, nodding. "You see, Mr. Oakwood, figs are actually inside-out flowers. And flowers get pollinated by insects. Like bees. Or wasps."

Mr. Oakwood opened his mouth to respond. Instead of words, out came a burp.

Nervous giggles rippled through the classroom. Megan giggled too.

"Some wasps crawl deep inside certain figs, like a caducous fig. They crawl so deep into the narrow opening that their wings and antennae break off. But that's okay, because they don't need to leave ever again."

"How do you know all of this?" Mr. Oakwood said. He burped again. A stream of liquid dribbled down his chin. It was kind of brownish red.

"My dad's an entomologist. He studies insects."

"I know what an entomologist is," Mr. Oakwood snapped.

"He studies wasps, you know. He breeds them downstairs in our basement. He has all kinds of specimens."

Suddenly Mr. Oakwood clutched his stomach and let out a high-pitched shriek. Other kids in the class did the same. They'd never seen their mean old teacher looking or acting like this before.

Megan didn't shriek. She knew exactly why Mr. Oakwood was clutching his stomach like that. She leaned forward. "Did you know I found out the combination to my dad's aquarium lock? It was pretty easy. He used the letters of my name. That was awful nice of him. And since I'm such a good watcher, Mr. Oakwood, I knew the exact strain of eggs to take out."

"Eggs?" Mr. Oakwood croaked. He could manage only the one word, and then he had to cover his mouth with his hands.

Megan nodded. "Some wasps, after they crawl into figs and lose their wings, will lay eggs. The eggs live inside the fig. The fig goes into somebody's stomach. The stomach is warm and toasty. Just what those eggs need to hatch. What you may not know is that it's not one or two baby wasps that are born. It's tens, maybe even hundreds."

Mr. Oakwood burped again. His eyes went wide. He opened his mouth.

Lewis Stoller pointed and screamed.

Something crawled out of the corner of Mr. Oakwood's mouth. Something with six legs, a striped body and a set of slender wings.

The creature buzzed and flew off. In its place, crawling out from the corner of Mr. Oakwood's mouth, were three more.

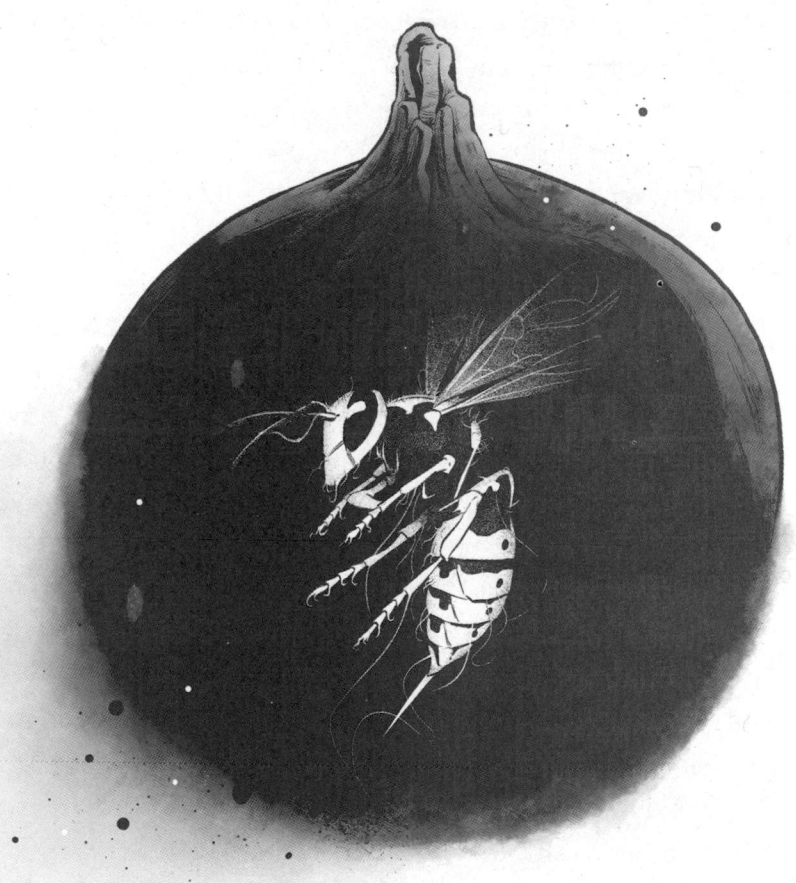

Mr. Oakwood's eyes were wide and bulging. Wasp after wasp flew from his mouth. He clutched at his throat. Megan knew he must be feeling the wriggling of dozens of the insects crawling up his throat, rubbing their wings together as they buzzed their way to freedom.

Megan knew better than to scream or start running, like the rest of her classmates were doing. You had to be careful around stinging insects. Sure, maybe one or two of her class-mates would get stung. But what if you had two hundred living inside of you?

In a few moments it was just Megan and Mr. Oakwood sitting at the front of the room.

The teacher gargled out a strained cry. Megan shook her head. "Oh no, Mr. Oakwood. You don't want to move. Or even scream. That will only make them angry."

Megan looked past Mr. Oakwood. The room was filling with a cloud of busy wasps. They wriggled into nooks in the wall. Some of them were chewing up the papers on Mr. Oakwood's desk.

Megan understood wasps. Some species, like those pesky humans, only seemed to look out for themselves. Some humans, like Mr. Oakwood, were cruel and greedy. Wasps were not greedy. They were fierce, they were brutal, but they always looked out for their queen. Wasps were a species Megan could get behind.

A dozen or more wasps came to land on the smooth skin of her arms. She kept perfectly still. She could feel them wriggling under her sleeve. Their legs tickled the hairs on her skin as they made their way up. She looked back at her teacher. His entire body was covered with a thick blanket of living, buzzing insects.

"There's nothing to worry about, Mr. Oakwood, as long as you keep *calm*."

THE PAPER CUT

Mike and Jerry had better things to do than listen to Mrs. Taylor drone on about making text-to-self connections to their reading. Jerry was trying to come up with an excuse to leave the classroom for the fifth time that day. Nothing made him want to skip class more than Mrs. Taylor and her mind-numbing lessons. He pushed his chair back and stretched his legs. Mike leaned across the desk in the next row and flashed a big grin.

"I bet I can make a better paper airplane than you," said Mike.

"You're on!"

Suddenly the two boys were tearing papers out of their notebooks. Mike folded his into a standard dart plane. Jerry turned his into a weird, multisided origami-style flier.

Nobody noticed them doing this. Not Mrs. Taylor. Not even Makayla, who sat closest to the two boys.

Mike eyed Jerry's plane. "What is that supposed to be?"

"Dunno," said Jerry. "I learned how to make it from some website."

"It looks ridiculous."

"Yeah, but bet you I can fly it to the other end of the room," Jerry said.

On the count of three, both boys flung their planes along the narrow gap between the desks and the window.

Mike's dart plane loop-de-looped and bounced off the window.

"Aw, crap!" he said.

Thankfully, everyone else in the room was still paying attention to Mrs. Taylor.

Jerry's plane, meanwhile, somersaulted through the air, gaining velocity as it did so. With an impressive burst of speed, the plane collided with Mrs. Taylor's desk. The paper shattered like glass into pieces.

"Whoa!" Mike said. "I didn't know paper could do that."

Jerry nodded. "It *was* a pretty cool website."

Mike looked over at Mrs. Taylor. She was still deep in her lesson, and so were the rest of the students. Either she hadn't noticed the two boys or she was purposely ignoring them. It was one of Taylor's tricks—she didn't give into Mike's or Jerry's antics until after the bell rang. But then she often grabbed them as they headed out for recess and made them stay in.

"Let's quit while we're ahead," said Mike.

Jerry nodded.

But then he ripped out another sheet of paper. He started folding it madly.

"What are you doing?" Mike whispered.

"The website showed how to make another airplane. But it gave some kind of warning too. So, obviously, I have to give it a test flight."

"What do you mean, **warning**?"

"I don't know exactly. The website was in some other language."

"Then how do you know it was a warning?"

"Well," Jerry said, folding as he talked, "there was a big, flashing, red bar with some word written on it. And there were pictures of people folding airplanes, with red lines through them like on those No Smoking signs."

"Then why are you making it?"

"You think I'm going to let some lame internet sign keep us from having fun?"

Jerry finished folding the paper. The plane almost looked like a blade, something that could really hurt somebody if it was thrown.

"This is not a good idea," Mike muttered.

"I know. Check me out, dude," Jerry said. He fired off the airplane.

At first the plane looked like it was going to sail right across the room and onto Mrs. Taylor's desk. But then the razor-sharp nose of the plane veered and seemed to slice the air in half, like a knife cutting through butter.

"Wha—?"

The plane disappeared through the incision. All that was left was the classroom. Only now there was a vertical slit around five feet in length in the space between the desks and the window. It made the world around it flap back and forth as if it were on a flimsy sheet of plastic wrap.

Through the slit was nothing but darkness.

It was a shade of darkness darker than any kind of dark Jerry or Mike had ever seen. It was so dark that their eyeballs and brains were not fit to process how dark it was.

"Uh-oh," Mike said. "Now you've done it."

"What **is** that thing?" Jerry asked. He also wondered why nobody else in the class had noticed the giant tear. But a tear through what, exactly? The classroom? The universe?

Jerry clutched his head. His brain was in overdrive trying to process what he was seeing. He turned away from the rip in the universe. The other students were staring at the board at the front of the class, copying down whatever it was that Mrs. Taylor was busy writing onto it.

"It's a black hole," Mike suggested, shaking his head at the impossible tear in the universe. "Has to be."

Jerry turned back to the hole, making sure not to stare directly into it. "If it was a black hole, it'd probably suck us in."

"But it's so…dark in there."

"You know this is all your fault," Jerry told Mike.

"My fault? How do you figure that? **You** threw the plane."

"You should have stopped me."

Mike rolled his eyes.

"We're going to get in so much trouble," Jerry said. "We'd better fix it."

"Fix it? Dude, you've created a giant void. Nothingness. Absolute nothingness."

Jerry nodded. "That's why we'd better fix it. I *can't* get another phone call home. I'll be totally grounded."

Mike was baffled. "How do we fix it then?"

Jerry slipped out of his seat and dropped to the floor. Nobody really took any notice of him as he scurried across the linoleum tile, crablike, until he was at Mrs. Taylor's desk. He reached up with his hand and fumbled around until his fingers clasped the stapler.

Meanwhile, Mike eased over to Makayla's desk. She was busy watching Mrs. Taylor. She didn't notice as Mike reached into her desk and fished out the big roll of masking tape she had brought for her science project.

Mike inched back to his desk and then joined Jerry over by the large slice. The edges were billowing like curtains in the breeze.

Once he had it between his fingers, Jerry tugged at the edges of the tear. It felt freakishly thin, like some sort of stretchy material. He ran his other hand along it too. Taking a deep breath, he plunged his hand through that deep, dark middle. His hand passed through empty space. Then Jerry craned his neck around the other side of the tear. The rip was still there too, only Jerry couldn't see his hand poking through the other side like he expected. "This is really cool," he whispered.

"Just hurry up," Mike said nervously. He turned to the front of the class, where Mrs. Taylor had finished writing on the board. The other kids were still staring. Mike turned away and pulled a length of masking tape off the roll. He tried to stick the two sides of the tear together. The tape held, but now the piece of masking tape was hanging in the air. Not good.

Jerry grabbed the stapler and started to snap the two sides together.

"This is never going to work," Mike huffed.

"Stop complaining. We'll just pretend we weren't the ones who did it," Jerry said. He pulled tightly on one edge, so it stretched past the sliver of jet blackness, and stapled it to the other edge of the tear. "What we really need is a good sewing machine."

"What are you two doing?" a voice boomed.

Suddenly all eyes were on Jerry and Mike.

"Uh, nothing," Mike said.

"It doesn't look like nothing," said Mrs. Taylor. She was eyeing the rather noticeable rip in reality. The random pieces of masking tape and bad staple job had left several long flaps of the universe overlapping with one another.

"Oh, that?" squeaked Jerry as he tried to make his way back to his desk. "That's...uh..."

"In the middle of my lesson, you've been tampering with the very nature of reality, haven't you?" The teacher took a few steps forward.

"We were just making some paper airplanes," Mike said. He sounded a bit whiny.

"And now you've gone and torn a hole with one," Mrs. Taylor said with a frown. "Do you have any idea what you've done?"

"Uh..." Jerry said.

"Erm..." said Mike. He turned away from Mrs. Taylor. The words on the blackboard behind the teacher's desk caught his eye. As he began to read, his eyes went wide.

Jerry pulled a long piece of tape off the roll. "Don't worry, Mrs. T. We can *totally* fix this."

"Oh yes," Mrs. Taylor said. "It will most certainly be fixed."

Jerry noticed that all the students were now staring at Mike and Jerry with wide, expressionless eyes. "Hey, Mike, what's up with the rest of the class?" he said.

But Mike wasn't looking at the students or at Mrs. Taylor. He was still staring at the board. "*My mind is not my own,*" he mumbled, reading from the board. "*My mind is not my own.*" It had been written on the board at least thirty times.

"That's right. Your mind is not your own," Mrs. Taylor said with a big smile, "because it belongs to me." She gave the shoddily repaired tear in the fabric of the universe a closer look. "I see you found my website."

"*Your* website?!" Jerry looked shocked.

"*My mind is not my own,*" Mike said, unable to take his eyes off the board.

"Don't mind him." Mrs. Taylor's smile got even bigger. "He's just being a good student."

"What language is that website even in?"

Mrs. Taylor cocked her head back and opened her mouth. Out spewed a mechanical sound, like a garbage truck compacting an old refrigerator into a small metal cube.

"Oh," said Jerry. He was pretty sure they didn't teach that language in this school.

"*My mind is not my own,*" said Mike.

Mrs. Taylor took Jerry by the hand and pulled him across the linoleum tiles of the floor. She had a firm grip. "I'm a little tired of teaching," Mrs. Taylor admitted. "I thought I would go home for the weekend."

Standing in front of the tear in the universe, she peeled off the masking tape and pulled the two sides apart.

Jerry stared into the depths of the tear. "You...live in there?"

"Beyond it," Mrs. Taylor said. "I admit it's a bit of a journey."

Jerry nodded. He was feeling a mixture of fascination and horror. He'd never been through a portal to another universe before, especially for the weekend. "Can we stop and get a snack first?"

"All taken care of," Mrs. Taylor said, turning the corners of her lips into a creepy grin again.

Sometime later, Mike blinked and looked around the room.

The rest of the students were also sitting at their desks, blinking. There was writing on the board, but the words had been smudged out. Mike's head felt a bit like it had been smudged out too.

Then he noticed something. "Hey, where's Mrs. Taylor?" he asked Jerry.

Jerry did not respond.

Mike turned to Jerry's desk, but it was empty. He shrugged. Jerry was always wandering off. He'd probably turn up soon enough.

TWENTY-FOUR
FRAMES PER SECOND

"You're getting rid of all these movies?"

Sam stared in disbelief at the trash bin behind the old movie theater. It was overflowing with torn-up movie posters and metal canisters containing reels of film.

Mr. Lambert, the theater manager, loomed behind Sam's shoulder. He had led Sam out here and was now pointing to the trash. "Every last one," the manager said. "Ever since the movie studios started releasing their films digitally, I have been losing business. Now I have to close down because I can't afford one of those newfangled digital projectors."

Sam noticed that Mr. Lambert's eyes were red, and his wrinkled face was covered in a wispy gray beard, like he hadn't had time to shave in a few days. His cheeks were hollow, and his skin hung down in loose folds.

Seeing the manager like this made Sam sad. Sam had visited this movie theater dozens of times, especially on Saturday afternoons when the manager screened old horror movies back to back.

"But why are you putting them in the trash?"

"I sold what I could to film collectors. This is all that's left. *Junk.* I have to clear out the theater by next week."

Sam swallowed. He wasn't sure how to ask the question, since Mr. Lambert seemed so morose. Nevertheless… "Um… can I have one?"

Mr. Lambert shrugged. "Unless you've got a 35 mm film projector, you won't be able to watch them, but be my guest."

Sam just stood there. The manager's sad face had vanished. Even the man's gray beard seemed to have shrunk back into his cheeks. A curious expression had taken over his ancient face. "You don't know how film works, do you?"

Sam shrugged.

Now there was a gleam in the old man's eyes. "Come in, and I'll show you. Last chance to learn the old ways before the theater closes down for good."

Sam shifted his weight from one foot to the other. He was supposed to go straight home after school. "I really shouldn't."

"Aren't you curious how all those old movies got made?"

Sam knew you weren't ever supposed to go anywhere with strangers. But he wasn't going anywhere weird, like following this guy into his car. It was the Paradise Theater.

He'd been there a gazillion times. And if there was some kind of problem, he'd run back out. The theater was open. There were people inside. "Okay," Sam said.

Mr. Lambert led Sam around to the front of the theater. The marquee there had probably looked great when all the light bulbs were working, but half of them had burned out. But Sam could still read **NOW PLAYING: NATHAN'S STORY**. Sam had never heard of that flick before. No wonder this theater was going out of business!

The manager waved casually to the cashier at the ticket booth, an old lady who looked as ancient as him. Sam got a bit of a thrill as they strolled right into the lobby, without even paying.

As soon as he passed through the glass doors, the smell of buttered popcorn hit him right in the nostrils. Looking around, Sam could see the place needed some work. The red carpeting stretched across the floor like a dry tongue, the middle worn down to only a few threads. Hunks of wallpaper were pulling off the walls like overripe banana peels. And the framed faded posters of old movies were cracked and chipped. Sam wasn't sure he'd ever seen the theater in such a sorry state. Sure, it had been a while since he'd been here— he mostly watched movies on his laptop or at the multiplex at the other end of town now—but man, this place looked rough. And like it hadn't been vacuumed in at least a decade.

Even the people working at the food concessions were as withered as raisins. They almost appeared to be coated in cobwebs. Sam had to narrow his eyes and stare to make sure he wasn't seeing things. Mr. Lambert took Sam by the arm and pulled him forward. "You don't want to stick around here, do you, kid? I thought you wanted to see how the movies worked."

Sam nodded. He sure did. He hadn't come all this way just to look at the snack stand. Even if the snacks looked kind of old. And when he gave the popcorn in the big glass popping machine a second glance, he could have sworn it looked more like a pile of wriggling maggots than something he'd want to eat.

The manager was really pulling on him now. Sam glanced back. The people at the snack stand were all staring at him intently.

A blur of movement caught Sam's eye. The door to the theater swung open, and a frail man—almost skeleton thin— stuck his head out. He stared at Sam like the snack-stand workers had.

Sam squinted and strained to see past Skeleton Man to the screen in the background. It wasn't a new movie that was playing, but some old black-and-white feature. The light from the screen was bright enough that Sam could make out most of the audience. They were all old. Very old and paper thin. Sam wondered if they were on a field trip from the old folks' home. Who else would want to watch this ancient film?

Sam didn't have time to really think about it. Someone called out, presumably addressing the skinny man by the door. "Hurry back. He's seen you!"

Sam saw a fearful look on the skeletal man's face—like he'd been caught in the act of **something**. The man abruptly turned away, letting the theater door flap shut. Sam wondered what the big deal was.

He thought about doubling back to the theater, but the manager took Sam by the hand and led him up a flight of stairs to the projection booth. He dug in his pocket, fished out a set of old, clanking keys and opened the door.

The booth was cramped. Canisters of film lined the walls. Long strips of film were stuck to pegs along another wall, beside a strange-looking machine built into a rectangular table. On its surface were spools and dials and a pair of reels connected to a small screen. In the middle of the room, a large projector clicked and hummed as two reels of film whirled and jiggled around like the back wheels on a Mack truck.

The manager beamed. "It's quite something, isn't it?"

"Huh?"

"Twenty-four frames per second. Each frame of the film is a still image, but string it through the projector and the images come to life." He pointed through a window in the booth that overlooked the theater.

Sam studied the projector. The reels were connected, so the film ran in a continuous loop. That didn't make any sense, did it? Would the movie ever stop? "The movie just keeps playing over and over again," Sam said curiously.

The manager pursed his lips. "I was wondering when you'd notice," he said.

Sam stared past the glass separating the projection booth from the theater. The old black-and-white flick looked pretty boring. On the screen right now was some kid, maybe Sam's age, standing there looking sad. The print was old and scratchy, like it had been run through the projector two million times. The image was all faded, too, so it was hard to make out much of anything other than the sad kid.

Sam looked down at the wrinkly audience. "Why do they keep watching it?" he asked. He couldn't understand why anyone would pay to watch a movie like this. It was obviously an old movie, but no classic that Sam could recall. Still, there was something about that sad-looking boy that held Sam's attention. Maybe it was just that there were no cutaways to anything else. It was only the image of that boy.

"Don't pay any attention to *them*," the manager said. "Let me show you the editing table."

He motioned to the machine against the far wall. It was one of the few pieces of equipment in the room, aside from the projector, that wasn't coated with an inch or two of dust. "We call this a flatbed," the manager said. "It's used to edit the film together, especially when it breaks."

Sam turned away from the bizarre image being projected below. He stepped toward the flatbed table and turned one of the reels. A light flickered on the screen. "What's it for?"

"When the film breaks, I have to repair it."

Some of the strips of film tacked to the wall beside the table were cleanly cut, others torn right in the middle of an image. Sam removed one of the torn strips and held it up to the light coming from the projector bulb. He could tell it was an image of the same kid being projected on the screen right now. But it wasn't in black and white. It was in full color and looked brand-new. That was weird.

"What's this?"

"Just a bit of film I shot," Mr. Lambert said.

Sam wondered if he had also shot the footage playing on the big screen. He noticed Mr. Lambert pick up something from the table. Sam turned. It was an old movie camera.

The manager pointed the camera at Sam. "Say cheese!"

"Huh?"

"Good enough!"

The manager pressed a trigger-like button. Even over the heavy clunking coming from the projector, Sam heard the film spin through the camera. The manager held the camera steady and aimed the lens right at Sam's face.

"That's right, give us a smile!"

Something was wrong. Sam knew he shouldn't have followed this strange man into a movie theater by himself. And it had been a bad idea to come up to the projection booth, where it was only the two of them. But it was more than that. The sound of the film running through the camera made Sam dizzy.

He blinked.

It must have been a long blink, because when Sam opened his eyes, Mr. Lambert was huddled over the flatbed, threading a piece of film through the machine. He hit a button and the film advanced through the spools.

The small screen connected to the flatbed editor lit up with an image that made Sam's blood run cold. It was *him*, Sam, here in this place! He was staring right at the camera that the manager had pointed at him. The film kept moving, and Sam kept staring. He had no memory of doing this.

Sam's muscles tensed. Mr. Lambert must have hypnotized him somehow, taken this movie and—now what? Edited it? What for?

Mr. Lambert didn't appear to notice Sam anymore. Or maybe he just didn't care.

Sam slowly backed away from the manager, but he slipped on the filmstrips that littered the floor like autumn leaves. He crashed right into the projector, knocking his head hard. One of the reels fell right off the projector. It clattered to the floor and unspooled before Sam's eyes.

Sam grabbed the film and held it to the light. He stared at the strip of faded images. The boy in those frames had been hypnotized too, just like him.

Where was the boy now? What had happened to him?

The manager switched off the projector. He stretched out a bony arm. Sam lunged to get out of the way, but the manager wasn't after Sam—he was after the strip of film.

Sam watched in terror as Mr. Lambert yanked the strip from him and spooled it onto the reel. Then he turned to Sam and licked his lips with a dry, white tongue.

Without breaking his stare, the manager slid the reel back onto the projector and turned it on.

Then he backed away from Sam and looked through the window to the big screen.

Sam got to his feet. He looked at the white light from the projector bulb shining through the window and out into the theater. The new image appeared on the screen below.

Sam stared through the projection-booth window. He was gazing at his own image. But it wasn't in black and white like that old movie that had been playing before. This time it was in full living color.

"It takes time for the film to lose its color," the manager said. He wasn't looking at Sam. His eyes were wide and unblinking. He was staring at the screen and taking in long, deep breaths. He was gulping in air the same way his eyes were taking in the movie of Sam playing on the screen.

"What's happening?" Sam sputtered.

"Didn't you ever want to be a movie star? Well, now's your chance. You're a part of the movie now, kid. Up on the big screen for everyone to see." The manager beamed. "Twenty-four frames per second. Looped over and over again so it keeps playing you to my audience. That other film is finished, you see. The color is drained. The projector creates too much wear and tear. The sprockets rip the frames apart. I can only fix the film so many times, and then it's trash."

He motioned to the wraith-like people below. They had been splayed across the seats, but now, with the new color movie playing, they were sitting up straight again, on the edges of their seats. Sam saw their eyes bulging, like they were trying to take in as much of the movie as they could.

"We're so very hungry," Mr. Lambert said. "You truly are a welcome feast for the eyes."

Sam felt sick. Hot bile rushed up his throat. He had to get out of there. He turned and shot his hand out to clasp the doorknob.

But his hand went right through it, like it wasn't there—

No. The **doorknob** was there. It was Sam's **hand** that had turned ghostlike, passed through the solid matter of the knob.

Sam whirled around. He stared helplessly at Mr. Lambert, who somehow looked much younger now, his face rounder than it had been before.

Sam opened his mouth to scream, to let out the loudest, most piercing shriek he could muster. But no sound came out. Not even when he tried filling his lungs to the max.

Mr. Lambert shook his head. "Sorry, kid. My camera doesn't capture sound. But the audience doesn't mind. They've been around since the days of silent films, and it suits them—and me—just fine."

A while later the theater doors opened. About twenty people filed out into the dull gray afternoon, rubbing their eyes as if they had been asleep for days or even years.

They were dressed in clothes that looked like they were from another time altogether. They helped brush the dust and cobwebs off each other's old-fashioned suits and frilly dresses.

As a group they stepped away from the theater, away from the marquee above that read *NOW PLAYING: SAM'S STORY*.

In the theater, the film looped through the projector.

And looped.

And looped.

And—

TWO BRAINS, ONE ALICE

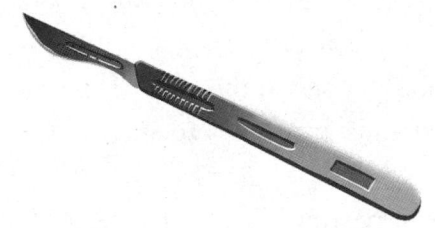

Alice barely noticed the brain at first. It was pushed against the curb, half buried under a blanket of dried leaves and garbage. It was the sort of thing you'd only notice if you happened to be walking home from school with your head down. Even then, the odds of actually spotting it were pretty remote.

But Alice had stopped, and her head was down. She studied the half-hidden object lying before her. She was still trying to figure out what it was exactly. It definitely resembled something she'd seen before.

Then her own brain began to piece the puzzle together. What Alice was looking at was an actual **brain**. A shiver of horror seized her. Alice checked over her shoulder. It was not a busy street, and there was nobody else around.

Just her and the brain.

A brain. A real human brain, the kind you'd see in movies or textbooks or even in jars at the museum.

But whose brain was it? And how did it get here? These two questions bounced around in Alice's brain while it juggled a third and the most important question: **Why?**

Alice became aware that she was disobeying her first instinct—the right instinct—which was to walk away, find an adult, and call the police.

Instead, she stepped to the edge of the sidewalk and got down on her hands and knees to stare at the disembodied organ.

It was like inspecting fresh roadkill. Alice recalled the first time she had seen a dead animal on the road. It was a squirrel that had been crushed under the wheels of a car. The sight of its guts smeared across the blacktop was enough to put her off eating her pizza that night. In fact, it had taken a week for the memory to fade enough for her to have more than a few bites of her meals. So why on earth was she now crouched over what was clearly a human organ without an owner?

But Alice continued to ignore her own brain, which was screaming, *Get up and walk away!*

Here she was, on all fours, her face so close to the brain that she could almost lick it. The brain was soft and gray, so fragile without its protective skull. She eyed the bumps and grooves. Alice was convinced it even jiggled under her breath. It was a miracle the thing hadn't been gorily dashed across the street like a hurled egg.

And whatever you do, DO NOT touch it!

Alice continued to ignore the warnings coming from her own brain.

She reached forward and pulled a dried-up leaf off the brain. The leaf was coated in a slick fluid that had probably oozed out of the organ. Then Alice found herself plucking more bits and pieces of garbage away, until she was staring down at the whole brain.

There was no brain stem to go along with it, no trace of any spinal column or the vertebrae that brains were normally attached to. Whoever had removed this brain had done so with the precision and care of a master surgeon. So why leave it here on the side of the road?

Alice was **certain** it had to have been left here. You didn't just toss a brain in the street and expect it to keep its shape. Come to think of it, the brain couldn't have been left alone like this for too long. Otherwise, ants and flies and other creatures that broke down living things would have got to it by now.

There were no bugs around the brain. Alice wondered if someone had deliberately hidden the brain on the street. Again, this only begged the question: **why?**

It doesn't matter why, *Alice. It's a human brain. Whoever put it here might still be close by. Might even be watching you. You need to get out of here now!*

But Alice had already picked up the brain and cradled it in her hands. It was cold and slimy.

And all hers.

Picking up the brain and taking it home with her—had that been her idea? Hadn't she wanted to walk away and tell someone?

Perhaps. Or perhaps not. Maybe the wrong sort of people would come for the brain. The police would take it with them to a coroner's lab. The brain would be cut up and dissected into pieces to help the police answer their questions.

Alice knew nothing of police procedures. Her parents never let her watch any of those forensic crime shows. Nevertheless, Alice had a picture in her head now of a cold metal table and men standing over it with scalpels and white surgical masks.

The thought punched right through her, as if it was one of her own.

Wasn't it?

Alice looked at the brain nestled gently between her fingers like a small animal. She wondered how she could get it home without being seen.

Alice's parents never checked her backpack. She always brought it straight up to her bedroom, because the first thing Alice was supposed to do when she got home was at least twenty minutes of homework.

Safe in her room, Alice unzipped the backpack and reached inside. She'd squished her books to the bottom of the bag, leaving a sizeable space for the brain.

She pulled the jiggly mass out as gently as she had placed it in the bag, trying hard not to bump it against anything. The brain didn't do well with sudden jostles or moves.

Alice carried the brain to her bedside table and placed it beneath the lamp. Then she dug back into the bag and pulled out her math textbook and notebook.

Alice sat down on her bed and groaned. Why did teachers always assign math homework? Probably because it was easy for them. The questions were already in the textbook, and the teachers had the answers ready-made.

But actually answering the questions by herself? Not so simple.

Math and science had never been easy for Alice. Even reading didn't come easily. It had taken her much longer than the other students to be able to read out loud without stumbling over each and every word on the page. Even in her head, she struggled with the longer words.

Math and science were *full* of longer words.

Alice flipped her textbook open and began to pore over the pages her teacher, Ms. Hoyle, had assigned. The first question had something to do with n plus 1 equaling 15. So what was s if $n + 1 + s$ equaled 19?

Alice huffed. Who wrote this garbage? Who cared what n or s equaled?

Her teacher cared, and, by extension, so did her parents. Her parents were the gatekeepers to Alice getting her allowance and time outside with her friends. So the more quickly Alice got her homework done, the more time she would have for other things.

Alice tried to think of the solution, but even the question was making her anxious. She stretched out her hands, like she always did when she got frustrated, and her fingers brushed against the side of the brain.

Fourteen, Alice thought, n is fourteen.

Another thought occurred to her just as quickly and just as reasonably: s is four.

Alice nodded as she mentally played around with the numbers a second time, watching them fit where the letters *n* and *s* had been saving places for them in the equation.

Then Alice glanced at a few more questions in the textbook. She blinked. Normally the words and images and numbers on the page tended to blur into one pile of gobbledygook. Not now. It was as if someone had stuck a pair of magic glasses over her eyes. Alice blinked, then zipped through the questions as easily as she might tie her shoes.

When she'd finished the work Ms. Hoyle had assigned, Alice turned the page and continued working.

Might as well get this work done while I'm on a roll.

She whipped through the next few pages in only a few minutes. She wondered briefly at her newfound speed and effectiveness. The doubt was a nagging tug at the corners of her thoughts. Something was wrong. Alice didn't get her math homework done this fast, this quick, this *easily*, ever.

But she was also confident—certain even—that this math homework was child's play. She continued to flip through the book, eyes scanning the words and numbers for something more challenging. But the textbook now felt to her like something she'd give to a toddler.

There was a knock at the door. "Alice? Are you coming for dinner?"

Dinner already? Alice looked up from her work. "In a minute, Mom!"

She put down her pencil, closed the textbook and looked over at the clock on her bedside table. She'd been working steadily for an hour and a half.

Her eyes dropped from the clock down to her left hand. It was still touching the brain.

Of course, Alice brought the brain with her to school the next day. But this time she was prepared. She'd found some Styrofoam packaging in her basement and had reinforced the brain with bubble wrap, so the organ wouldn't get bumped around while she walked.

The brain, Alice determined, needed a challenge. It wasn't a muscle, but much like a muscle, the brain needed to be flexed. And so what if it helped her with her schoolwork? What did that matter?

She raised her hand when Ms. Hoyle asked if anyone wanted to review the previous night's math homework in front of the class.

Ms. Hoyle gave a surprised blink. "Really, Alice? The algebra?"

Alice, who had put her bag under her desk and was now touching the brain, smiled.

Ms. Hoyle thinks I'm a dummy.

Alice removed her hand, wiped the brainy slime off on her pants and marched up to the board. She ignored the guffaws and snorted laughs bubbling up around her. They all thought she was a dummy, Alice realized, but that wasn't going to get in the way of things this time.

Normally, when Alice found herself at the front of the class, her knees knocked and her breath got ragged. She hated having to stand in front of others and not be able to do anything right.

But today she plucked a piece of chalk off the ledge and twirled it between her fingers like you would a key.

She turned to her peers, saw their silly grins and—

POW!

Alice blinked. She stared at the sea of faces, but they weren't her classmates. Not the ones she was used to seeing.

Instead, Alice was staring at a group of students in old-timey school uniforms, sitting at sturdy wooden desks. They were staring and laughing too.

It was a memory, all right, but was it Alice's? She couldn't tell. She knew the names of the students, especially that redhead in the front: Derek Michaelson. He was looking her way and taunting her. "Curry's in a fury! Curry's in a fury!"

Curry?

Her name was Alice.

But this must be *Curry's* memory, she decided.

Alice blinked and—

The other students were gone, replaced with her own classmates. They sat in their chairs, staring at her.

"Well?" a voice called out. Alice followed the voice to Ms. Hoyle, standing a few steps away from the board. "Are you all right, Alice? Do you need some help?"

Alice took another moment. Moving from the memory to the here and now was disorienting, like spinning around and trying to walk straight afterward.

Alice shook her head. Then she turned around to face the board and started to scrawl the answer to the homework question.

She was done in less than a minute and had even explained her thinking. She turned around to face the class.

It was Ms. Hoyle's turn to stand there. She looked like she'd been hit by a bus. Finally she spoke.

"Alice, that's…*amazing*."

Alice put the chalk down on the blackboard ledge and secretly smiled. Starting from now, things were going to be a lot different for her.

After school Alice turned her backpack around so the pack was strapped to her front. That way she could unzip it and look down at the brain on her way home. She only unzipped the top part of the bag, so no one else could see the organ contained within.

Alice stared into the grooves and fissures that lined the surface of the brain.

It pulsed like a heart. Like a complete organism.

No. This was not right. But she couldn't look away either. The brain wanted Alice to place her hand on it.

Wanted her to.

Needed her to?

Alice's hand pressed against the slimy surface of the brain.

And she *remembered*.

Remembered looking up from the cold metal table. The men and women (it was hard to tell who was who under those white surgical masks) were standing over her, holding sharp metal scalpels.

Alice exhaled.

That's not your memory, she told herself.

But it was. And enough with this **Alice** business. Gilbert was her real name.

His name.

It was the brain, Alice realized. *You're touching the brain, and the brain is sharing its own thoughts with you. And its memories. Brains shouldn't be able to do that. They're not living things. They need human bodies. Without a body, a brain is just a piece of meat.*

Alice breathed in and out heavily. Sweat beaded on her forehead and clung to her skin, making her shirt stick to her back.

But she kept her hand firmly on the brain, because wasn't that what the brain wanted her to do? She felt it throb against her wet palm. Its pulsing matched her own, and other memories bubbled in her thoughts.

His name was Gilbert. Gilbert A. Curry. Images came with the name. Of a boy growing up into a man, studying hard. Always studying. Always working. Learning the big words in math and science books.

Neurosurgery—the cutting and fixing of the brain. That was Gilbert's job.

Another image. It felt like a memory, but Alice wasn't sure whose.

The image was of a house. It was a house on a street she passed every day on her way home from school.

It was the house on the street where she'd found the brain.

Alice looked up.

She'd been walking without paying attention, but now she stopped. She pulled her hand away from the brain and rubbed her fingers. They were slick with sweat and the fluid that oozed from the gray organ.

She stared at the house and shivered.

It wasn't a particularly scary house. It looked like all the others in the neighborhood, with a tree in the yard in front of it. The grass was green, and there were flowers in a patch of earth beside the porch. It was a normal, everyday house, nestled among lots of other normal, everyday houses. And *that's* what made Alice shiver.

Alice didn't think twice about stepping off the sidewalk and walking up the path to the front porch.

She remembered this house as if it were her own. She knew that the front-door key was under the potted plant to the left of the front door. Sure enough, she lifted the plant and there it was. Exactly where Gilbert had always left it.

Alice twirled the key in her hand, because that's what Gilbert liked to do. Then she pushed it into the keyhole and opened the door.

Stepping inside, she found the house exactly as she'd left it.

No! her brain screamed. *You've never been here before! Get out! Get out while you can!*

Alice reached into the backpack, placed her hand on the brain, felt it pulse and felt the screaming in her own head disappear. Yes, she decided. The house was *exactly* as it had been left before.

She strode through the front hallway. The kitchen was still in order, and those dishes that had been left in the sink still needed cleaning. Then again, there were always dishes in the sink that needed cleaning. Gilbert was not one to tidy up right away.

But it was not the kitchen she was interested in.

Alice strode over to the door next to the kitchen and opened it. She looked down into a shaft of darkness, then reached over and flipped on a light.

A carpeted stairwell led to the basement.

Down she went. The basement was anything but creepy. There was carpeting, the walls were painted bright yellow, and pictures hung on the walls. One picture in particular interested Alice. It was a large, framed photograph of an old man with a wild shock of hair and a thick mustache. The word below it proclaimed: **EINSTEIN.**

Albert Einstein. Alice nodded. She didn't need anyone else's memories to explain who *he* was. The famous scientist who had come up with his own equation: $E = mc^2$.

Equations like that had never made much sense to Alice, but now that she had her hand on the brain, energy equaling mass times the speed of light made perfect, plain old sense.

Still, the image itself did not interest Alice.

Her interest lay in what was hidden behind it.

Alice felt behind the large frame. There was a small gap in the wall. She got up on her tippy-toes, squeezed her fingers into the space, felt the latch and flipped it.

Then Alice stood back as the framed picture slid aside as if on a set of rollers. The picture was now hanging a couple of feet to the left. In its place was an open doorway.

Get out of here now.

Alice put her hand back into the bag and massaged the brain. It was running low on fluid, she determined. But the solution was just a few steps away.

She hunched and stepped through the doorway.

Alice found herself in another room. Unlike the rest of the basement, this room was not carpeted. The floor was bare stone. A string of fluorescent bulbs flickered on above her, revealing metal shelves lining the walls. The shelves were full of various pieces of medical equipment, electronics and jars full of thick fluid and various human organs.

Brains, Alice noted. Brains in jars, just as Gilbert had left them.

Taking up the center of the room were what appeared to be two metal beds. Surrounding them were several stools, as well as carts loaded with other scientific apparatuses. Alice spied many sharp implements—saw blades, scalpels, knives. The metal gleamed under the lights.

It was a surgical station. Beneath it, on the cold stone floor, was a drain. Alice didn't need to run her finger along the edge of the drainpipe to know what she'd find there. Blood. A few dark pools on the floor revealed that the table had been used recently.

The memory flashed again. Alice—or was it Gilbert?—on the table, looking up at the faces under the white surgical masks and at the shining metal scalpels they held with precision.

Shaking off the memory, Alice looked over at one of the shelves and spied rows of vials full of a greenish fluid. The serum Gilbert had been looking for.

Alice strode over to the shelf, pulled out a vial and opened it. Then, after taking a sniff of the liquid to make sure it hadn't gone bad, she poured it over the brain in her pack.

The brain pulsed and squelched, sucking up the fluid.

Alice let out a sigh, as if she'd just guzzled down a glass of water on a scorching summer afternoon.

She now understood the importance of the serum. Gilbert had planned to introduce it into the local water supply. He'd had no time to turn the serum over to the Food and Drug Administration for review. They would want to test it. Some fearful scientists might not approve of his methods. But Gilbert was certain that the serum, if properly introduced, would change people's minds and the way they thought.

It would be a new scientific world. Everyone would have the opportunity to be a genius. A single dose of the serum would improve brain function dramatically.

But there'd been a hiccup in the plan.

Gilbert had had assistants, of course. But somewhere along the line, his helpers had turned as fearful of his ideas as the watchdogs in the drug administration. They'd reached a point where they no longer trusted Gilbert A. Curry.

Undoubtedly a genius, he was, nonetheless, too dangerous, they thought. So his followers decided to remove his brain from his body. They would stop Gilbert's maniacal plan while keeping his brain intact to preserve and learn from it.

Fools! They didn't know that Gilbert had already dosed himself with the serum. That the serum could keep the brain alive even after the body was taken care of. That Gilbert had taken so much of the serum, in fact, that he could also control other people's thoughts.

If an unwitting human placed their hands on the brain, or even stood close to it, Gilbert could exude his own will onto them. Of course, he'd taken enough of the serum to be able to do this, but other people wouldn't be allowed access to such a high concentration. It wouldn't do to give others the same power.

Gilbert had needed the power. Otherwise, those "helpers" of his might have taken control of his brain.

Still, his helpers had not been imbeciles. They were geniuses in their own right, and forcing them to bend to Gilbert's will had been no easy trick. There had been only enough time for Gilbert to suggest that they gently place his brain by the curb, away from the roar of traffic, before he erased their memories.

He'd been at the mercy of the elements then. Getting left on the curb wasn't ideal. Not good or safe. Animals might have pecked or nibbled at what was left of him, but he could keep them at bay for a short while. They were the easiest to control—the ants and flies and birds that would have otherwise devoured him.

He'd known it would only be a matter of time before someone found his brain just lying there—

Alice, you've got to get out of here.

Alice shook the words away as Gilbert's thoughts filled her own.

Only a matter of time, Gilbert determined, before someone found it, took it and nursed the brain back to health.

Oh, Gilbert would still need a body to complete his work. *Any* body would do.

The problem now was that there were two brains and only one Alice.

Alice, if you know what's good for you, you must go now. Back up the steps—

Alice stared at the metal tables, at the surgical equipment, and remembered. This kind of equipment was as easy to use as tying a pair of shoelaces.

Alice, please! Listen to yourself! Do you know what he intends to do to you?

Alice smiled.

Two brains, but only one Alice? That was no problem at all.

SCRATCH

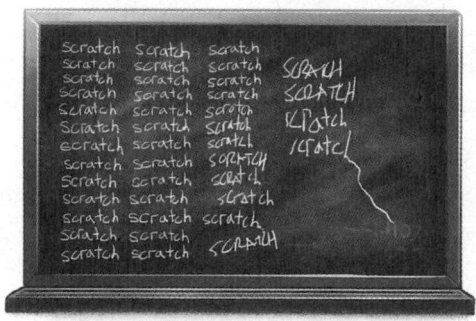

Avi figured he was a good enough artist that it was fine for him to scribble wherever and whenever he wanted. His sketch notebook was just the start. He doodled on desks or inside of textbooks when Ms. Fetch wasn't looking. Eventually he got daring enough to snatch one of the dry-erase markers and draw a picture of her oversized rear end on the whiteboard while her back was turned. He made sure to include stink lines coming out of her butt.

The gales of laughter he received were worth the phone call home and the detention he received the next day.

Avi's school was originally one of those one-room schoolhouses from pioneer days. You know, back when they crammed twenty kids from every grade into one room and had some old lady try to teach them all. Ms. Fetch looked like she was old enough to have been around since then.

The new school had been built up around the old schoolhouse, which was now used as the caretaker's storage area.

And the detention room.

Who even used a detention room these days? Wasn't that just for grumpy principals in those high-school movies from the 1980s?

That's what Avi was thinking as Ms. Fetch led him down the hall to the door with a sign that said **DETENTION ROOM**. The door had to be at least hundred years old, all scratched up with what appeared to be nail marks.

Ms. Fetch pulled out a thin key that looked like it should have opened a haunted house. She eased it into the keyhole, and Avi heard a heavy *click*. The door creaked open, scraping against a cold stone floor. Ms. Fetch flipped on the lights.

The detention room had been partitioned off and was no bigger than a large closet. There was space for a couple of chairs, a desk and a blackboard. Not a whiteboard, like in the new part of the school, but an old blackboard that you could only write on with chalk. The board had been wiped clean, but Avi could still see traces of writing on it. It looked like whoever had been here before had been writing lines over and over.

Avi followed Ms. Fetch inside and looked around. "So what am I supposed to do? Sit with my head on the desk?"

Ms. Fetch fished a piece of chalk from the ledge under the blackboard. Avi noticed that the ledge was full of dust, but there was only this one piece of chalk. It was small, about the size of a thimble. She handed it to him. "You draw."

Avi looked at her, confused.

"You heard what I said. You wanted to be an artist, so here's your chance. *Draw*." There was nothing inviting in the way she said it. She sat down in the second chair and waited.

Avi had no idea what to put on the board, so he wrote the letters of his name.

"No, not that."

"Oh." Avi thought for a moment and then wrote the words *I'M SORRY*.

Before he could even turn around to face Ms. Fetch, she stood up. "That's not what you were drawing in my classroom, was it?"

Avi didn't say anything.

"Was it?"

Avi shook his head.

"What did you draw in my classroom?"

"A picture."

"*A picture*," Ms. Fetch repeated, "of me."

Avi nodded. So *this* was where she was going. Avi figured he had to play it like he actually was sorry. "I'm sorry, Ms. Fetch. I'm really, really sorry. It won't happen again."

Ms. Fetch smiled and shook her head. "Now, we both know that's not true."

"It is true. I promise. I won't draw it again. I swear!"

"But that's just it, Avi. You're going to draw it again. Right now. For me."

"What?"

"You heard me. I am going to sit down, and you are going to draw that same picture of me. Right now."

Then Ms. Fetch sat back down in her chair, crossed her legs, folded her arms across her chest and waited some more.

Avi pinched the nub of chalk between his fingers. His hand trembled. His whole body was shaking. He didn't know why. He turned to the board and drew the picture as best as he could remember. He formed the outline of the body and—

"No, that's not it. You made my rear end *much* bigger."

Avi wiped away the line he'd drawn and made it bigger, rounder. But his hand was shaking so much now that the edges were wobbly.

"There you go. Just like that," Ms. Fetch said with a grin. She leaned forward so her enormous behind lifted away from the chair. "But you aren't finished yet. You forgot the best part."

Avi stared at her.

"The little wiggly lines coming from all around my body. You know, as if I stink."

"No, Ms. Fetch. You don't stink. I mean, you—"

"Do it."

Avi swallowed again, but his mouth was so parched it felt like his tongue was about to crack. He drew the stink lines. When the picture was all done, Avi stood back and looked at his handiwork. He got it. It wasn't funny to make pictures like that.

Ms. Fetch stood up and strode over to stand right beside Avi. She didn't even look at him. She leaned in and studied the picture intently. Then her eyes fell to the ledge below the board. It was full of white dust, obviously from other kids who had been forced to draw pictures or write other stuff for her. She picked up a pinch of the white dust, rubbed it between her fingertips and smiled. "Very good, Avi." She pointed to a blank space on the board. "Now draw it again."

"But I—"

She didn't interrupt him this time. She didn't need to. She simply backed up and sat down in her chair. And waited.

Avi drew the picture again.

When it was finished, Ms. Fetch surveyed it from her chair. "Excellent, Avi. You're getting quite good at this. Again."

Avi drew the picture again. By now, though, the little nub of chalk was turning to dust in his hand. He was only halfway through the drawing when his fingernails started screeching against the blackboard. The high-pitched squeal of his nails against the board made his body shake and goose bumps swell. His teeth chattered.

"I didn't say to stop, did I?"

Tears were forming in the corners of Avi's eyes. He had to take a deep breath to keep them from spilling onto his cheeks. "I'm out of chalk."

"Did you hear what I said?"

"How am I supposed to draw without any chalk?"

Ms. Fetch shrugged.

Avi looked at his hands. There was a bit of chalk on his fingertips and under his nails. It would have to do.

Biting his lip, Avi raised his hand to the blackboard and continued to draw the outline of his teacher. His fingernails screeched against the board. The sound and sensation tied knots in Avi's stomach. It was the same icky feeling he got from biting down on a hunk of tinfoil or pulling a popsicle stick across his teeth.

"You're doing a very good job, Avi. Keep them coming."

But Avi couldn't hear her. He drew that picture over and over. His fingertips burned. He kept scraping the picture onto

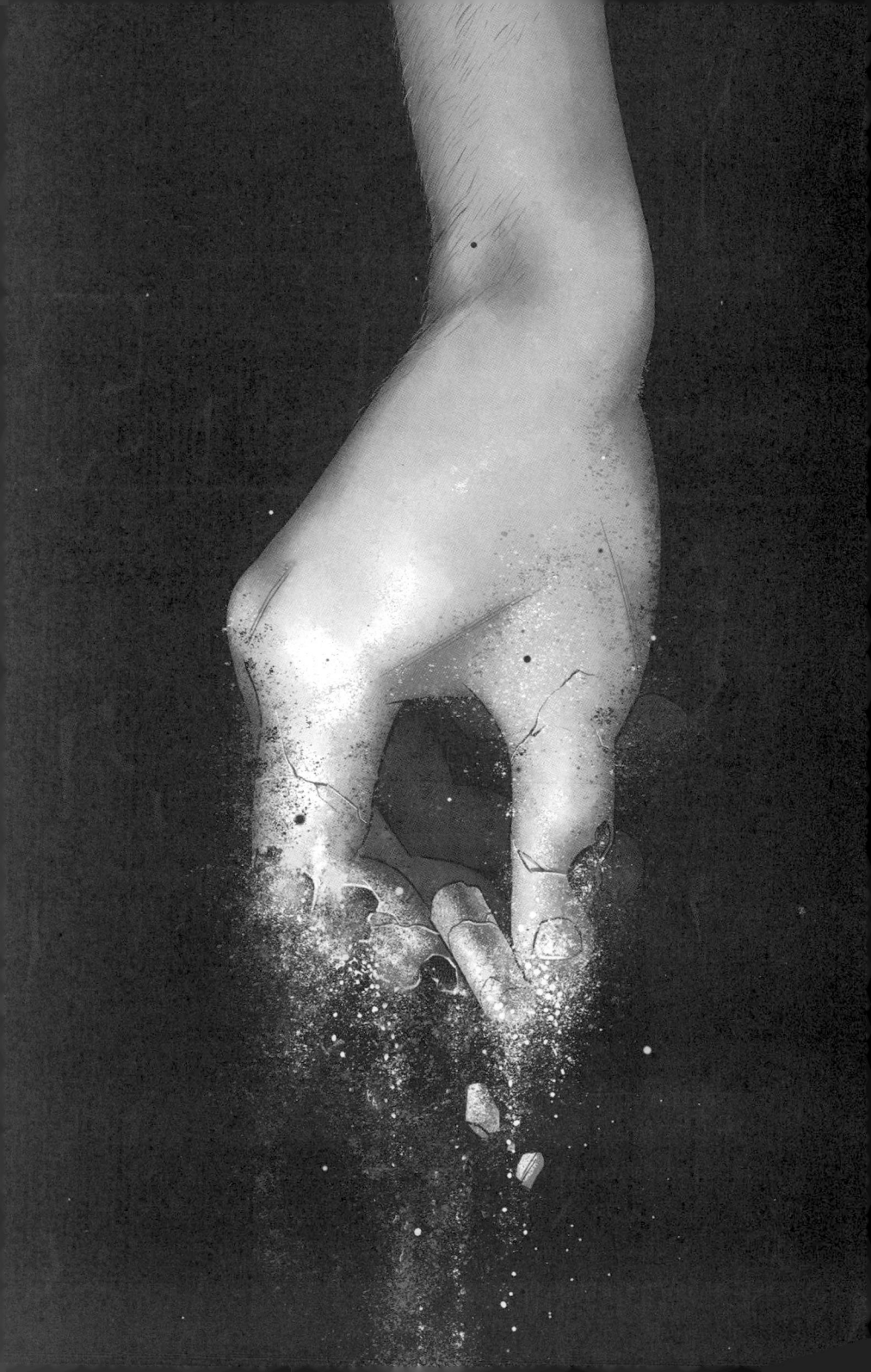

the board, watching as little flakes of white fluttered down into the ledge beneath the blackboard like fresh snowflakes.

The dust.

Avi wondered how much was chalk and how much was shredded fingernails. But it was hard to wonder over that horrible sound.

Sometime later, Ms. Fetch let him stop.

The next day Avi came to school with his fingertips in bandages. He'd worn his nails away well past his fingertips. Both hands throbbed with pain.

Avi had always wanted to be an artist, but he didn't feel much like drawing anymore.

He skulked at the far edge of the schoolyard, afraid to get close to the school, even though he knew he would have to go in there sooner or later.

That's when Avi noticed his friend Jaiden wandering around with his head hanging down. Jaiden didn't look so good either. Normally he'd be out playing soccer with the guys on the field.

"Jaiden, what are you doing here?"

Jaiden shrugged.

"Well, you'll never believe what happened to me after Ms. Fetch caught me drawing." Avi told him everything that had happened, how Ms. Fetch had made him scratch his own fingernails off against the blackboard.

Jaiden opened his mouth and smiled. Or tried to. Avi was horrified to see that Jaiden's teeth didn't fit together the way they used to. There was a huge gap in Jaiden's smile, and Avi could see all the way into his mouth.

"That's nothing," said Jaiden, saliva dribbling all down his chin. "Ms. Fetch made me *eat* my own words!"

WHISKERS

Greg took a deep breath and jammed the scoop into the kitty litter. He raised it and watched the sand trickle through the gaps. A residual dark wet clump rolled back and forth. His lungs about to burst, Greg gasped for air and started to gag. Wow, that cat sure could stink up the house!

Two months earlier she had followed him home from school.

At first Greg hadn't minded the company. He had friends, he supposed, but they were the kind of friends who existed only when his parents set up play dates. *Let's go see the Baldersons*, his mother would say. And then he would get stuck playing some dumb video game with Aaron Balderson, who had clearly mastered it some time ago and was only playing it because he enjoyed destroying Greg in every way possible. Greg would sit there and grumble while his parents were upstairs having a great time, laughing with Aaron's parents.

And then one day he'd heard a feeble "meow" from the bushes.

Part of Greg's walk home from school took him past the ravine. You weren't supposed to go into the ravine on your own, because it was too steep. All the parents in the neighborhood warned their kids that they could trip, break an ankle and get stuck down there. Or worse. This had actually happened to a few kids over the years—kids had wandered into the ravine and then couldn't get back out. Greg remembered walking home one time and seeing the street by the ravine cordoned off with yellow caution tape. The street had been packed with police cars, fire trucks and an ambulance. Greg couldn't make out the details through the flashing red lights. Maybe he didn't want to.

But the day he'd found the cat, the street along the ravine was calm as usual. There had been no police, no firefighters and no ambulance. Just a pathetic mewing from behind a thatch of tall grass by the side of the path leading down to the ravine. Greg had dropped to his knees and peered into the foliage. A small cat carefully poked her head through the bush and then jumped out and landed on the sidewalk by Greg's feet. She was white, with orange and black calico patches. Her tail swished back and forth like a rudder. The cat looked up at him and meowed.

"Meow yourself," Greg had said. He got up and started heading home. He had made it about half a block when he heard it again.

"Meow."

The cat was still following behind. She quickly caught up to him, looked up and purred.

Greg bent down. The cat didn't have a collar. Most cats he'd seen did, in case they got separated from their owners. Not this cat. She just stood there, purring and staring at him with her big eyes. She pawed at his shins like she wanted something. Food, perhaps?

The cat had followed Greg all the way home. Greg told her to get lost and went inside. But the cat stayed on the front steps, meowing, until Greg's mother came home from work.

"What's that cat doing here?" she had asked.

"Good question."

He told his mother about the cat following him home and refusing to be shooed away.

His mother smiled. "I've always wanted a cat," she said.

And so Whiskers was part of the family now. Greg's mother had named the cat. While she clearly enjoyed having Whiskers around the house, she wasn't as excited about cleaning up after her. That job fell to Greg.

Greg took another breath and fished around the litter box for any other presents that Whiskers might have left for him. He felt the scoop connect with something hard and shook the sand away. A flash of chrome shimmered back at him. Greg frowned.

There was a key in the litter box.

Greg got a weird feeling that someone was watching him. He turned. Sure enough, the cat was peering out from behind a leg of the kitchen table. Whiskers blinked at him a few times, then rubbed her head against the table leg, marking it with her scent.

Greg plucked the key out with a thumb and forefinger. He wondered how it had got in there. He imagined Whiskers trying to eat it, but how would that jagged piece of metal make it through a cat's digestive system? Perhaps it had fallen into the box somehow. Then he realized he was holding something that had been sitting in cat pee. He flung the key across the floor and quickly finished cleaning out the litter box.

Whiskers padded out from behind the kitchen table and approached the key. She sniffed at it, then looked up at Greg, blinking her eyes a few more times. "Meow?"

Greg took a paper towel from the sink and used it to pick up the key again. He ran it under the tap and wiped it off with a fresh paper towel.

Whiskers did a few figure eights around his feet. "Meow?"

"You are *so* weird," Greg said to the cat. He put the key on the kitchen table and went upstairs to do his homework.

"Why is there a key on the table?" Greg's father asked when they all sat down for dinner.

"Isn't it one of ours?" his mother replied.

Greg explained where he'd found it.

His father laughed. "How did Whiskers manage to get

this into her litter box?" He dangled the key before the cat. "You find this outside, kitty? You giving Greg some buried treasure? Huh, kitty-kitty?"

"Meow," Whiskers replied. Greg could have sworn the cat sounded annoyed.

Greg's father set the key down on the tiled floor. Whiskers quickly approached it and then batted it in Greg's direction.

Greg's father laughed.

"That cat is hilarious!"

At 7:00 AM Greg's alarm clock blared to life. His hand automatically shot out to turn it off. He felt something cold and jagged under his fingers. Whatever it was slipped off the top of the clock radio and thunked against his night table.

Greg rubbed the sleep out of his eyes and blinked the world into focus. He pulled the covers back and reached over. His fingers found the cold, jagged thing. He knew what it was without looking, but he held the key up to his face anyhow, so his eyes would be satisfied.

Greg lowered his hand. Whiskers sat at the foot of his bed, washing herself. Greg looked from the cat to the key and then back to the cat again.

Whiskers purred and hopped off the bed.

Whiskers was waiting on the front steps when Greg got home from school. She lifted a paw to greet him. Greg bent down to

scratch the spot behind her ears. He stopped scratching when he saw the key. *Again with that key!* Did she think it was a toy? He regarded it uneasily. "Did you bring this out here?"

"Meow."

Greg sat down, his head full of questions. Whiskers stuck her bum into the air, stretched her forelegs and then hopped down the steps and across the driveway. She paused by a sidewalk and gave Greg a sideways glance.

Greg wrinkled his brow. "What, you want me to follow you or something?"

"Meow."

The cat trotted down the sidewalk. Without removing his backpack, Greg pocketed the key and followed Whiskers down the street.

Every so often the cat stopped and looked back, as if to make sure Greg was still following. Greg soon recognized the route—it was the way he walked home from school every day. A few kids were still slowly ambling to their homes. Some cars passed, but the street was quieter now than during the afternoon rush.

Whiskers finally stopped. When Greg caught up, the cat did a few figure eights around Greg's legs.

Greg picked up the cat and looked around.

He was standing by the ravine, in the spot where he had found the cat.

"Meow." Whiskers pawed at Greg's chin. He put her down, and she immediately scampered away, disappearing through the thick grass.

"Whiskers!"

Greg waited for her to return. A few more cars passed by. From somewhere in the thick forest beyond came the call. "Meow."

How was he going to explain this? They'd only had the cat for a short time, and already she had run away. Greg's mom was going to freak out.

Unless he went down there and brought Whiskers back.

Greg stepped past the bushes, then suddenly stopped. The ravine dropped down steeply fifty feet or more. Overhead foliage blotted out all but a few patches of sunlight. There was a small creek at the bottom, where Greg could see a small white animal lapping at the sparkling water.

Whiskers.

Greg tried to step down sideways, but his foot slipped, and he landed on his butt. He felt the mud seeping into his pants and cursed. Whiskers, finally noticing him, slowly turned and traipsed along the ravine floor, disappearing around a bend in the path.

Greg took hold of some tree roots protruding from the mud and pulled. The roots extended deep into the ground, and they would hold Greg's weight just fine.

Slowly, carefully, he made his descent.

"Whiskers! Where are you?"

Greg held his hands to his mouth to amplify his voice. He'd been down here for half an hour at least. His clothes were dirty. Sweat had made them stick to his skin. He was going to have to give up looking for the cat soon and get back home. His parents would be wondering where he was.

He told himself he would round one more bend along the path at the bottom of the ravine and then give up the search for that day. Who knew? Maybe Whiskers would follow him back home again. Maybe she'd even be waiting for him at the foot of the front steps.

Around the bend Greg spotted an old wooden shed wedged under a few mature trees. It wouldn't have been visible from the top of the ravine, as the trees hid it from view. The only way to actually see it was to be down here at the bottom.

Standing majestically at the door was Whiskers.

Greg breathed a sigh of relief and splashed through the puddles to scoop up the cat. He no longer cared that he would be walking home with a pair of soakers.

The cat safely in his arms, Greg took another look at the shed. It wasn't much bigger than the kind of pre-made backyard shed you might find at a hardware store, large enough to hold maybe a small bench with some tools. There were no windows.

What the heck was a shed doing here?

Curiosity got the better of him. He put Whiskers down, hoping she wouldn't run off again, and inspected the shed more closely.

"Hello?" he asked. "Anyone home?" He knocked on the door. There was no answer.

Whiskers nudged the door. "Meow."

"Is there something in there you want?"

A latched bolt had been fixed to the door. A heavy padlock kept the bolt in place.

Whiskers stood on her hind legs and stretched, her front paws, reaching for Greg's pant pocket.

Greg stood there in disbelief. "The key?" he asked the cat, immediately thinking himself stupid for asking an animal to confirm his suspicions. "*This* key opens the door?"

Whiskers got back down on all fours, tail swishing behind her, and regarded him.

"Meow."

"How could you possibly know that?"

But the cat just stared patiently ahead.

Greg slid the key into the padlock. He gave it a twist and heard an audible click. "Hey, what do you know?" He smiled and looked at Whiskers again. She licked a paw and rubbed one of her ears. Greg removed the lock and slid the latch open.

He stood there a moment in front of that shed, alone in the woods. Well, not totally alone. Whiskers was there. But she didn't count. She was only a stupid cat.

Greg shrugged and opened the door.

Instantly he gagged. The shed smelled bad. He couldn't identify what it was that stank. Sure, there was the pungent odor of the old wood it was made from, and something growing and mossy. Maybe fungus?

No. It was more than that. The shed smelled of something organic. Like an animal. A dead, rotting animal.

But where? The cabin was dark. There were no windows. The only light that entered came from the door, now half-closed, and the tiny cracks between the wooden boards of the walls.

Greg stepped inside. The floor creaked.

What was that smell?

"Meow?"

"Not now, Whiskers."

Greg extended his arms, trying to feel his way around the shed.

His foot connected with something. Greg bent down and felt a familiar texture—denim. But these jeans were wet. Greg pulled his hands away and ran his thumb over his fingers. Now his hands were cold and sticky and smelled bad.

As his eyes adjusted to the low light, Greg began to make out more lumps, all of which appeared to be clothing. A few pairs of pants. Some shoes. And shirts. And jackets. And—

"Meow."

She was licking the wet stuff from his fingertips.

"Whiskers, *please!*"

Greg pushed the cat away, trying to take it all in. That's when he realized the clothes weren't strewn about aimlessly. They'd been pieced together, almost as if they were meant to be worn as sets of clothes. All they were missing was their owners. So what was holding them together?

Gingerly Greg reached out his hand and touched the jeans again. He felt something solid inside and jerked his hand away. His stomach took a nosedive. "Oh no," he gasped.

He straightened quickly, his mind swirling with images of police tape and ambulances. He remembered the news reports about children who had gone missing in the ravine and never been found. As he made his way back to the door, his foot knocked against one of the shoes, taking it right off and exposing something withered. Something that had once been alive. In the dim light of the shed he realized he was looking at toes, only they were white and thin, with little speckles of red.

Suddenly the door creaked shut. Greg thought he saw something cat-shaped leaping away.

Heart hammering in his chest, Greg grasped the door. But it was locked. How could it be? He'd just unlocked it. But then he felt the familiar outline of the padlock.

The padlock was on the *inside* of the door?

Greg felt for the key he hoped would still be inside the lock. Nothing.

In the darkness, Greg could feel Whiskers circling around his legs in figure eights.

She was purring.

A KERNEL TAKES ROOT

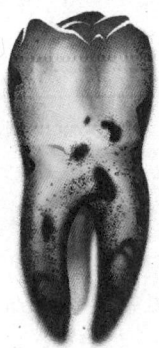

There was definitely *something* stuck between Jamie's teeth.

Jamie was pretty sure it was the husk of a popcorn kernel from the night before. He'd stayed up late watching scary movies and devoured that entire bag of buttery, puffed goodness.

It didn't feel like a whole kernel, just a piece of one that had popped open. It was lodged between two of his upper teeth and had been bothering him all day. Every time Jamie swallowed, his tongue brushed against the sharp edge of the kernel, slicing his taste buds.

Kernels were the *worst*! Oh, Jamie supposed they had some kind of purpose. Everything had a purpose. Without kernels, there would be no seeds for the corn to take root. Without corn, there would be no popcorn. And without popcorn, what kind of scary-movie night would it be?

By the end of the school day, Jamie's tongue was raw and swollen from grazing the kernel's razor-like edge.

It bothered him all afternoon and during dinner and all evening. When it was time for bed, Jamie realized he was going to have to break out the dreaded dental floss. He marched up to the bathroom, pulled a long stretch of waxed thread off the roll and wound it around his fingers until the tips turned white.

He stared at his reflection in the mirror. "Where are you?" he asked, studying his open mouth hard to locate the kernel. A dark blotch between his incisor and cuspid caught Jamie's eye. *Aha!* He raised the length of floss to his mouth, pulled it tight and shoved it between his teeth.

"Gotcha!"

Jamie pulled the floss back and forth through the narrow gap between his teeth. As soon as that darned thing popped out, Jamie would spit it down the drain and never be bothered by it again.

But suddenly the floss snapped in two. A mix of saliva and food bits spattered against the mirror.

Jamie frowned. He took half of the used floss, wrapped it around his fingers again and tried to rid himself of the kernel once more.

And once more the floss snapped.

Was there something to this flossing business that Jamie wasn't getting? He wedged the last piece of floss between his teeth and pulled sharply on it. The floss shot up and sliced against his tender gums. Jamie let out a yelp of pain.

Again the floss was severed. Dejected, Jamie pulled out the two bloodied strands and tossed them to the floor.

He leaned toward the mirror and bared his teeth like some kind of tormented animal. Where was that kernel? Did he need to get a toothpick? See a dentist even? Jamie shuddered. If there was one thing he hated more than flossing, it was the dentist. That was because the dentist didn't just floss but also took out the sharp-pointed scraper and dragged it against Jamie's teeth. The thought alone gave Jamie goose bumps. Unfortunately, this was a job that only the scraper could handle. Jamie was sure of it now. He was—

Jamie stared at his reflection in the mirror. He blinked and then stared again. Somehow he could see the kernel now, like the thing had moved. Like it had pushed itself to the front of his teeth. Or *grown*.

Jamie ran his tongue along the kernel one more time, and yes, it caused him pain, and yes, the thing felt bigger.

He tucked his throbbing tongue to the back of his mouth and leaned closer to the mirror.

With a shaking hand, Jamie dug his fingers into the corners of his mouth and pulled his lips open.

It wasn't a kernel. Jamie could see that now. The thing wedged between his teeth was growing right before his eyes. And Jamie knew what it was.

It was a tooth.

A new tooth, to be sure. But not like any of his own. This one was yellow and twisted and sharp.

Not a tooth then. A *fang*.

Growing fangs was plain ridiculous. It wasn't real. It was the kind of thing you imagined after staying up late and eating far too much popcorn.

Jamie decided to simply ignore the fang for now. Maybe it would be gone in the morning. Maybe this was just his brain playing tricks on him. He rinsed his mouth one last time to wash away the blood, turned off the light in the bathroom and went to bed.

He pulled the covers up to his neck. He was feeling a little bit dizzy. The skin on his face seemed cold and clammy. Maybe he was coming down with a cold or some kind of virus.

Jamie turned off his bedroom light and drifted into a dreamless sleep.

The alarm clock blared to life.

Jamie opened his eyes. Sunlight streamed into his bedroom through gaps between the blinds. He pulled himself out of bed and let his feet thud against the floor with greater force than usual.

What was the first thing Jamie did in the morning? Brush his teeth.

It was all part of the routine that had become automatic. Jamie's mind could wander, and his body would go about the routine without taking in all the details—walk down the hall, open the bathroom door, pull toothbrush and toothpaste off the counter, stick toothbrush into mouth—

Jamie spit out a mouthful of toothpaste at the mirror. He wiped it away with his hand, smearing the glass.

The fang had **grown**.

It hadn't just grown in length but had swelled in width too. It easily dwarfed Jamie's other teeth. It hung so low now that it threatened to puncture his lower lip. It had forced his other front teeth aside as if they were paper. The fang was twisted and rutted, and Jamie could see a layer of yellow scum covering the surface.

Jamie wiggled the fang. He wondered if it might come loose, like a baby tooth. He stopped cold before he could form another thought. He could feel the very roots of the fang burrowing farther up into his gums, anchoring deeper into his flesh. The tooth lengthened like pulled toffee.

He had to tell Mom and Dad. It would mean a trip to the dentist, but what was a needle and the drill compared to this dagger in the middle of his mouth?

Jamie stormed downstairs, prepared to tell his parents what was happening. But they were preoccupied with getting Jamie's kid brother packed up for school. His father had his work pants on but was still wearing the T-shirt he'd gone to bed in. His mother's hair was wrapped in a towel. Everyone was scurrying back and forth with the typical frenzy of a weekday morning.

Jamie opened his mouth to tell them everything.

Tried to open his mouth.

He could feel a force preventing him from flexing his jaw. It clamped that hinge shut like a vise. Jamie swallowed. He wiggled his jaw, cleared his throat and opened his mouth.

Before he could utter a sound, his mouth snapped shut like a clam.

"Good morning, Jamie," his father said. "Here's your lunch. Put it in your bag. And get dressed, will you? We're running late."

But I've got a fang, Jamie said—or tried to say.

Again his mouth resisted Jamie's attempts to expose the fang.

Jamie scow<u>led.</u> He could still write a message down on paper, couldn't he? Explain everything to his parents? They'd understand. Hopefully, they wouldn't think it was some kind of weird joke.

It was worth a shot.

Jamie turned and ran back up the stairs to his bedroom. He pulled a sheet of paper from the printer on his desk, fished around for a pencil and began to scrawl his message.

I GREW A FANG. IT CAME FROM A POPCORN KERNEL THAT WAS STUCK BETWEEN MY TEETH. IT WON'T LET ME SPEAK TO YOU. GET ME TO A DENTIST!

Jamie looked at the note and nodded.

Then he looked up.

He was staring into a mirror on his wall.

His mouth opened without Jamie even trying.

A second fang had grown beside the first, pushing Jamie's other teeth back out of reach.

"What...? How...?"

He stopped cold.

The fang *lengthened*.

And then it spoke.

Of course, it was Jamie who was doing the speaking. It was his own mouth moving, his own jaw jutting back and forth. Wasn't it?

Even the voice sounded like his.

"You will want to resist," Jamie said to himself, only the words weren't coming from his own thoughts.

He opened his mouth in horror, tried to scream, but the tooth took over. "They *all* try to resist at first…"

Jamie resisted. "Wh-wha-wha…what. D-do." He had to tighten the muscles of his mouth and work against the forces that were pulling on his own jaw and face. "What do you mean, *all*?"

But instead of an answer, Jamie felt the roots of the fangs work their way deeper into the flesh of his face. They seized control of the muscles around his cheeks, causing his lips to curl into a horrid smile.

Jamie wasn't surprised that the tooth did not want him to talk that day, even when he got to school.

Normally, he'd be chatting up a storm with his friend Hamid. The pair of them had spent the entire year trying to come up with new and creative ways to irritate their crusty old teacher, Mrs. De Palma. Not that this was hard to achieve. Mrs. De Palma got irritated by almost everything, especially children. Jamie couldn't figure why she'd chosen teaching as a career.

It didn't help that she was the most boring speaker Jamie had ever heard. Her voice was either a dull monotone

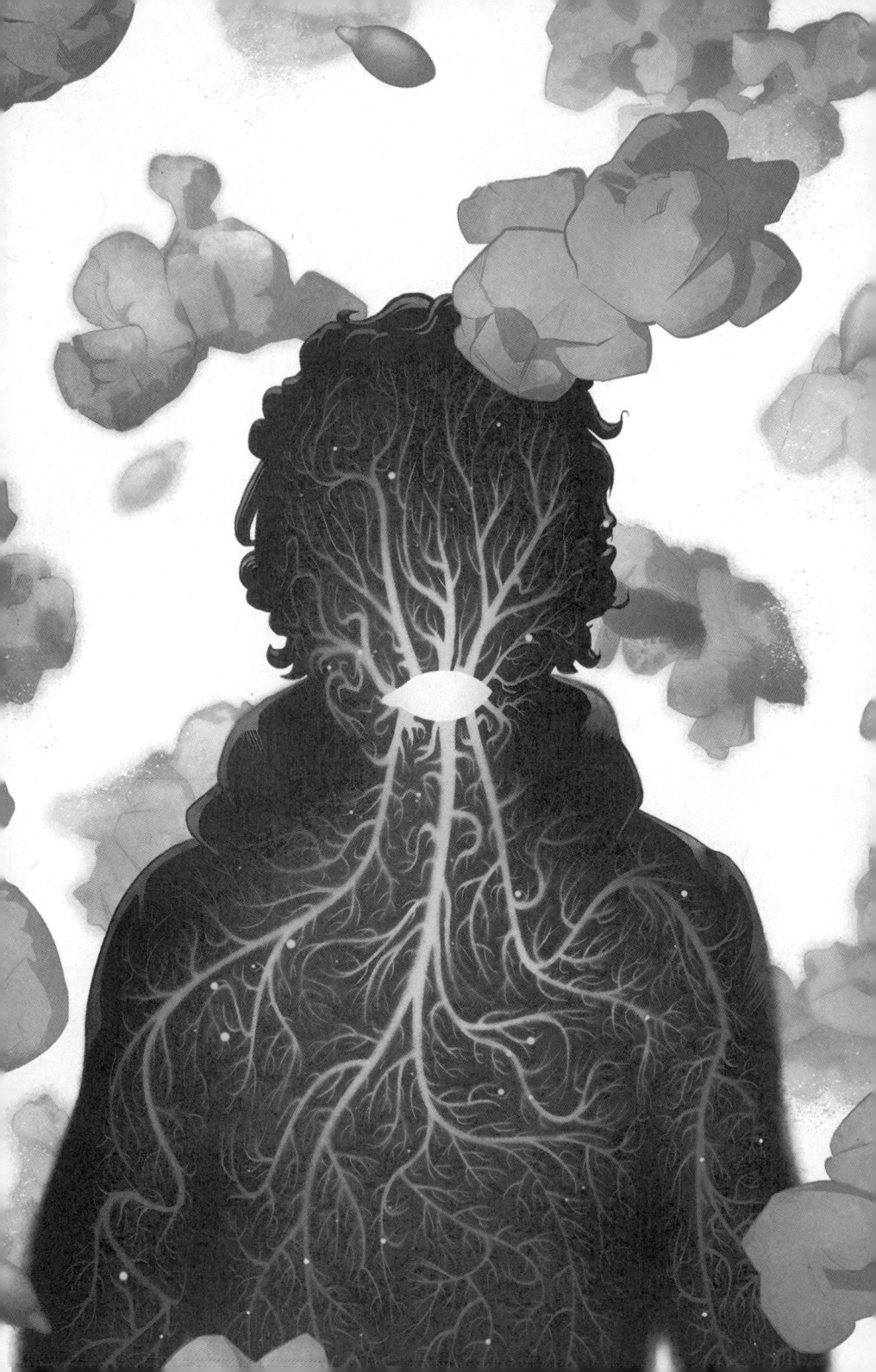

(when she was in a good mood) or a nasal screech (when she was upset, which she usually was with Jamie). It was always "Blah, blah, blah, practice your spelling words," or "Blah, blah, blah, study for your math test." That morning Mrs. De Palma was busy explaining how to write paragraphs. It took her a long time to write down the words on the front board, since she made sure each letter was perfectly printed. That gave everyone else in the class plenty of time to pass notes and whisper to their friends.

"Pssst."

Jamie turned to find Hamid holding what appeared to be a long red ribbon with a series of raised dots running down the middle of it.

"Check these out," Hamid said. "They're explosive rounds for my dad's old cap gun. We can set them off in the class when De Palma's not looking. We can even take that magnifying glass on her desk and concentrate a beam of sunlight on them. I bet that might set them off. Either way, it'll be *hilarious!*"

Hamid thought almost everything that involved spoiling Mrs. De Palma's class was hilarious, and usually Jamie would agree.

But that morning Jamie just shrugged, keeping his mouth firmly closed. How was he supposed to tell Hamid about the fang-like corn kernels growing in his mouth? What would Hamid do when he saw them?

Maybe it was worth a shot. Jamie tried to open his mouth, but the teeth held his jaw tightly together. How could they do that?

Jamie tried to murmur the word *help* through his closed lips, but Hamid shrugged.

"I know," Hamid said. "It's gonna be awesome!"

Jamie tried again. "Hlllllllllp mmmmmmmm!"

Then he reached into his desk and pulled out his writing book. He started to scrawl the words **HELP ME**, but he made a mistake with the **P**. He was about to erase it when a dark shadow fell over his desk.

"What's that you're writing?"

Jamie looked up to find Mrs. De Palma staring him down. Her face was contorted into a furious scowl.

"I will not tolerate such filth in my classroom," she said with a huff. She gestured to the open door. "Please leave at once," she said. "We will discuss this matter later."

But I need help! My mouth is being taken over by fangs growing from a piece of a popcorn kernel. That's what Jamie wanted to say.

But the kernel teeth in Jamie's mouth wouldn't let him speak. And Mrs. De Palma had nothing further to say.

Other students—basically, Hamid—had tried to put up a fight with Mrs. De Palma before. This had only brought them to the office, and a visit with Mr. Carpenter, the principal.

Jamie's biggest problem wasn't Mrs. De Palma anyway. He sulked out of the room and into the hallway. Across the way was the boys' washroom, as good a place as any to figure things out.

Jamie thundered into the washroom. His heart was hammering so madly he was amazed it didn't burst right out of his chest. He clutched his hair and spun around in a circle or two. He must have looked pretty messed up, because the two boys who were goofing around at the sink took one look at him, stopped what they were doing and immediately left.

Jamie staggered to the sink and clutched the cold porcelain edge. He hunched over it, feeling the world spin around him. Slowly he raised his head to look at his reflection in the over-size mirror. He had to stare through a thick film of soap and scum, but there he was. His face was bone pale, his eyes wide and bloodshot. Jamie swallowed, feeling a big, painful lump in his throat.

Then he dared to open his mouth.

For a second he thought the teeth weren't going to let him. But his lips pulled apart like the velvet curtains at the start of a play.

As Jamie had suspected, the kernel-fangs had taken over even more of his teeth, creating a jagged set of stalactites.

It was amazing they could even fit inside his mouth. Jamie stared at them with fascination and horror.

"Theresssss no way to connnnntrolll it," Jamie said, knowing full well it was not him but the teeth doing the talking. "Soon I'llllll havvvve the teeth. Then the tongue. Thennnn—"

Jamie clamped his hand over his mouth.

But the teeth sunk deep into the flesh of his hand, and Jamie yelped. A few drops of blood splashed into the white sink.

"Yesssssss," Jamie said, not even looking at his reflection but staring instead at the drops of red as they swirled around the drain. "Sssssssoon I shall have you all to myself."

But you're a kernel of corn, Jamie tried to say. Corn grew in fields and got popped and eaten. It didn't have a mind of its own. It was meant to take root in the earth of farmers' fields. Not in fleshy human gums.

Unless it wasn't just a kernel of corn.

Maybe it was something that only looked like corn. Something that had drifted to earth from another world. Like in that movie Jamie had seen the other night. Seeds and pods came down from outer space, and the pods took over people, made doubles of them and got rid of the actual people.

Jamie stared at the fangs again and shuddered.

"You are right to fearrrrr meeeeee," said the teeth.

A glint of sunlight shone in through the window and bounced off the exposed teeth. The reflected light created a noticeable glare on the mirror, and Jamie had to shield his eyes.

Jamie forced his mouth shut, whirled around and kicked open a toilet stall. He sat down on the toilet seat, ignoring the fact that it had not been wiped perfectly clean. He pulled the stall door shut, locked it and brought his knees up to his chest. He sat there, rocking back and forth, trying to think things through.

Jamie knew it was only a matter of time before the kernel would have taken over all of his actual teeth, one by one. And then what? He could feel the roots of the kernels burrowing farther into his face. Would they take his eyes next and turn them into unseeing yellow orbs? And after that? His ears? His nose? His mind?

The glint of light off the mirror had given him an idea, but he'd need help. And he'd have to wait until lunch.

Shortly after the lunch bell rang and Mrs. De Palma left the room, Jamie handed Hamid the note. It was as messy as a note scrawled in both terror and a hurry could be. But Hamid was used to passing notes and easily deciphered Jamie's hurried handwriting.

"Use the magnifying glass. Don't stop until they're all popped," Hamid read aloud. Then he turned to Jamie, who just sat there, nodding. "What do you mean, **until they're all popped?**"

But Jamie was already on his feet.

The rest of the class took no notice of Jamie as he skulked over to Mrs. De Palma's desk. They were too busy shoving food into their mouths or throwing it around the room.

Hamid followed Jamie. He watched with delight as Jamie started pulling open the drawers of Mrs. De Palma's desk. "Oh, I get it now. You want to go with my brilliant idea of using the magnifying glass to set off those caps!"

Jamie shook his head, fished out the giant magnifying glass and shoved it into Hamid's willing hand.

Then he pulled his lips apart to show Hamid what had to be done. He watched Hamid's face switch from excitement to something else. Hamid jumped when he saw the tangle of twisted kernel fangs that now took up all of Jamie's mouth. His fright shifted quickly, though, to amusement. "Nice one," Hamid said. "How'd you manage that?"

But Jamie didn't reply. Slowly Hamid's jaw dropped as he realized the infiltrating teeth were real after all. "What the—?"

"UURRRMMMM," Jamie mumbled and pointed to the magnifying glass. Then he pointed to the teeth.

"You want me to burn your teeth?"

Jamie nodded—or tried to.

"I think you need a dentist, Jamie."

But Jamie jabbed at the magnifying glass in Hamid's hand. Suddenly his lips pulled closed. The teeth **knew**.

Jamie yanked his mouth open again. Spit flew forth in a massive geyser.

Hamid jumped back, fear flooding through him.

"Ppppllleeeeeeeeeeasssse," Jamie managed through the forest of fangs. He threw himself back onto the desk, knocking over all sorts of marked papers, pencils.

Hamid swallowed nervously. He clutched the handle of the magnifying glass. He nodded. And then he held the glass up to the window, focusing a beam of sunlight onto Jamie's mouth.

Meanwhile, in the front row, someone pointed in Jamie's direction. "Whoa!"

That caught the attention of other students. "Jamie, your teeth!"

It took about ten seconds for the rest of the class to throw down their meals and rush to surround Jamie and Hamid at the teacher's desk.

"Sweet! Hamid's gonna pull another prank on De Palma!" someone shouted, beginning a round of hysteria from the students.

Hamid remained focused. He directed the hot beam along the yellow kernel fangs hogging Jamie's mouth. He stood there, transfixed by them. The heat began to change the fangs. They started to jitter in their sockets. Then they writhed like the legs of an angry, upturned centipede.

"What's happening?" Hamid heard someone ask.

"Popcorn!" Hamid said. "Jamie's got to get rid of the popcorn!"

And then a kernel exploded out of Jamie's mouth. It bounced off the whiteboard and rolled under Mrs. De Palma's desk.

Jamie screamed. Hamid screamed. Everyone else decided to join in.

"Popcorn! Popcorn!" The screams turned into a chant.

Jamie clutched at his lips, pulling them as far apart as he could. He could feel the teeth growing hotter, and hotter, and finally exploding out of his mouth. It was white-hot pain, but with each pop he could feel the kernels loosening their grip on him.

He widened his mouth even more and let out a scream of pain and triumph. Popcorn continued to erupt from his gaping maw, leaving gaps and holes where his teeth had once been.

"You cannnnnnnot stopppppp meeeeeee!" Jamie screamed. It was the kernel screaming through him, of course, but Jamie shook his head.

"Too late for you!" Jamie blurted. "It's too late now!"

"What is all this racket?!" boomed a voice so deep and sonorous that Jamie was sure it had erupted from the very bowels of the earth.

It was, in fact, Mrs. De Palma, standing at the classroom door.

"Popcorn!" came the excited screams.

She stared at the mess of popped corn piled up on her desk, then marched over to it, swatting at the children as if they were mice. They scurried back to their desks and watched from the safety of their seats.

Mrs. De Palma tore the magnifying glass from Hamid's shaking hands.

Hamid himself slid off the desk, nearly tumbling to the floor. His knees wobbled. He shifted his uneasy glance from Mrs. De Palma to Jamie and back again. "You okay, Jamie?"

Now Mrs. De Palma and everyone in the room fixed their gazes on Jamie, with the same level of intensity as the beam of sunlight that had burned out Jamie's fangs.

Slowly, surely, Jamie lifted his head from the pile of popcorn. The kernels seemed a bit glazed. A bit red.

Jamie's head bobbled unsteadily on his neck. He looked around at the popcorn carnage, then slowly, deliberately, opened his mouth.

The class screamed.

Jamie ran his tongue across a dribbly set of gums and understood why. *All* of his teeth were gone now.

The fangs, or whatever had last been in his mouth, were scattered across De Palma's desk, popped and puffy. He was definitely going to need the help of a dentist now.

Jamie slid off the desk, his mind spinning like a top. His mouth ached with a searing pain. But his brain throbbed with relief. He could no longer feel the kernel between his teeth, and not just because he had no teeth. Whatever had taken root in his gums had exploded out of him as well.

Out of the corner of his eye, he noticed Mrs. De Palma picking up a piece of the popcorn. She held it between her fingers and stared at it curiously.

"Stop, Mrs. De Palma!" Jamie exclaimed. "Whatever you do, don't eat that!" He said these words as loudly as he could, but without any teeth, all that came out were saliva-filled mumbles.

He watched as she dropped the popcorn piece inside her cavernous mouth and crunched down on it—

And then let out a yelp.

When Mrs. De Palma opened her mouth, that's when Jamie saw it. A kernel—a small piece of one, but big enough to be seen—was stuck between her teeth.

Oh no, not again!

Seeing the horror on Jamie's face, Mrs. De Palma waved him off. "Not to worry," she said. Jamie watched as she reached into her purse and fished out a blue spool. "I *always* carry dental floss."

CHEWY ONES

"Do I have to?" Alain whined, like he did every Halloween.

The response was swift and firm. "Now, please."

Alain rolled his eyes and slung the bag onto the kitchen table. A sea of colorful, cellophane-wrapped gems spilled out. Alain had filled a garbage bag with candy this year. The thing weighed a ton. He felt like Santa Claus on Christmas Eve, only this bag was full of candy, and it was **all his**.

At least, it had been before Mom and Dad started picking through it.

His mom dumped the bag on the table, the contents tumbling out and filling every bit of free space. Every

Halloween, his parents became obsessed with checking each treat to make sure the candies, chocolates, chips and whatever else he'd gathered were not poisoned, tainted or concealing bits of razor blades.

Alain was no dummy. He knew good candy from bad candy. But all he could do was stand and tap his foot impatiently as Mom and Dad sorted his loot into the Good and Bad piles.

It was like watching one of those TV documentaries about quality control in a factory, his parents stooped over the table, plucking out suspicious tidbits and eyeing them under the kitchen light above. "Nope," Dad said, tossing a loosely wrapped chocolate into the Bad pile.

"Not this one either," Mom echoed a second later, flinging a toffee with a slight bend in it.

"Those will stick to your molars. I bet a dentist handed it out."

"I read a study saying this brand of potato chip causes brain damage."

"And the preservative coating on this candy wrapper has been shown to cause disobedience in laboratory mice."

This went on for nearly half an hour. Mom and Dad had already gone through Jacqueline's treats. His kid sister had lost a third of her haul. All Alain could do was look on as his haul was whittled away piece by piece.

"What's this?" Mom asked, picking out a tightly wrapped object. It was round, maybe a chocolate or a gumball. The packaging was some sort of bright foil, a mixture of every color you could think of. As Mom rolled it in her open palm, the wrapper caught the kitchen light and reflected it into

Alain's eyes. It was mesmerizing to stare at. It made the kitchen start to spin so delightfully.

Alain reached out, not to eat it, but to touch it.

Mom snatched it away. "Not this one either, I'm afraid." She closed her palm.

Alain blinked once. Twice. His head cleared. "Why not?"

"I don't like the look of it."

Alain jabbed a finger at her. "You don't like the look of anything!" he snapped. "You ruin Halloween, that's what you do!"

"Alain," his dad said sternly, "we're only doing this to keep you safe. Haven't you heard what happens if you don't check your candy?"

"Yeah, you *enjoy* it!"

"That's it. Go to your room."

But Alain was already thumping up the stairs. He slammed the door and sat down on his bed, fuming.

Later that night, when his parents were asleep, Alain's eyes snapped open.

He'd been dreaming, but not the usual sort of dream. This one was only colors, like the kind he'd seen on that amazing wrapper.

Alain slipped out of bed and tiptoed downstairs. A bright shaft of moonlight slanting in through the window meant he didn't even have to turn on the lights. He didn't even need to eat the candy—he just wanted to see that wrapper again.

Once he got to the kitchen, Alain pulled open the drawer underneath the sink and peered into the garbage. He reached into his pocket and pulled out the small flashlight he'd brought from his room. He shone it into the garbage. It was a disgusting mix of candies and table scraps.

Alain plunged his hand in and stirred the garbage around. He pulled his slimy hand out, wiped it off on his pajamas and then shone the light back into the bag. A burst of color shimmered back at him. Alain smiled as the world around him dimmed. It was so pretty.

Alain plucked the round candy out of the stinky mess. The colors shifted like the skin of a chameleon.

He sat down at the table and peeled a corner off, revealing a dull white candy underneath. He took extra-special care to peel the foil without tearing it. Once he got it off, he spread it into a square. Then he noticed the smell.

It was coming from the candy. Like the wrapper's colors, the smell of the candy kept changing. First, he caught a whiff of cotton candy. Next, licorice. After that, a marshmallow odor. Alain was already salivating.

He knew better than to put things in his mouth that had been in the garbage. But it had been tightly wrapped in foil. There was no way any germs were on it, right? Besides, what could one little candy do?

Alain popped it into his mouth.

At once his tongue went into taste spasms. The candy danced from flavor to flavor. His senses had never experienced anything like this. Alain chomped down.

It was so chewy. Almost like a piece of gum. And the chewy ones were **the best.**

Each bite made him salivate more, and each swallow was a different delicious flavor.

It was almost too much, in fact. Soon Alain's sense of smell and taste were overpowered by the chewy morsel. He stood up and paced to the kitchen window. Pushing it open, Alain took a deep breath and stared into the night sky.

A stretch of clouds blanketed the full moon. There were other things in the sky as well. Birds, most likely, but they were so high up that to Alain they looked like flying ants.

Alain kept chewing. The taste was amazing, but it really was getting to be too intense. He opened his mouth to spit out the candy.

But it wouldn't leave.

Alain formed his lips into an O and tried to force the candy out.

It wouldn't budge.

The more he strained, the more the candy resisted. Alain took a deep breath and blew hard. But the candy changed form. It thinned into a balloon-like substance that bubbled out of his mouth.

Alain tried to pop the bubble. Although very thin, it was strong. Alain grabbed a knife from the cutlery drawer and tried to stab it. He jabbed and jabbed, but the bubble would not pop.

Alain began to panic. He started to hyperventilate. This just made the bubble grow. That gave him an idea. He put the knife down and started to deliberately fill the bubble with more air, hoping it would stretch and burst.

Instead, Alain felt his feet lift away from the floor. He was floating.

He dog-paddled with his arms, the way he'd learned in swimming lessons, but a gust of wind swept in through the open window. It twirled him about and then sucked him outside.

The current of air was strong. Helpless, Alain floated up past the roof, past the big old tree in the backyard. Soon he had a bird's-eye view of the neighborhood. How was he going to get down?

Alain kept floating. He thought about trying to suck the air back into his lungs to deflate the bubble and hopefully float back down. But he could barely breathe out his nose. He'd already pumped way too much air into the thing.

As he continued to rise, Alain got closer to the objects he'd seen flying around earlier. His brain struggled to process what he was seeing. The sky appeared to be dotted with a dozen or more other kid-like shapes. Each one had a large bubble sticking out of its mouth.

He shivered, and not just because of the changing temperature of the air as he rose.

Hovering above the floating kids were several other shapes. They were also human, but they were astride broomsticks, and they whizzed about the night sky like gleeful fireflies. They all had pointed hats and warty noses, and as they zoomed in closer, Alain could see that they were all smiling at him.

A few of the witches had spread a big weblike object between them. Alain watched in horror as some of the kids floated right into the net. They waved their arms wildly. He could hear their muffled screams through the big candy bubbles coming from their mouths.

Alain tried to paddle away, but eventually he, too, was caught in the net.

As he looked up at the big, bright moon, one of Alain's captors pointed at him. "Oh, look!" she said with obvious delight. "I bet that one's chewy! Don't you know the chewy ones are *the best*?"

LAST OF
THE DAVES

At first, I didn't think it was such a huge deal that Dave Anders had been away from class for four days.

Who didn't get sick for a day or two? One of those super-bugs could knock you out for the whole week. I figured that's what had happened with Dave. His seat was empty, and after the first day, Ms. Spector, our homeroom teacher, skipped his name while she took attendance. He was the first one on the list, alphabetically speaking.

I was last on the list, since my surname is Ziegler. Today Ms. Spector scanned the attendance sheet as she paced the rows of desks like she usually did. But when she got to my name, instead of calling out *here,* like we'd been trained to do, I raised my hand.

"Excuse me, Ms. Spector, but what about Dave A.?"

Because my first name is David too, Ms. Spector uses our surname initials to tell us apart.

My teacher looked up from the attendance list and blinked. "Dave A.? Who's Dave A.?"

"Dave **Anders**. He's in our class. He's the first on the list."

Ms. Spector looked at me as if I'd spoken to her in a foreign language. She stepped toward me and shook her head. "There's no Dave Anders on the list, David."

Nervous laughter rippled through the classroom.

I narrowed my eyes. Was this some kind of joke? "But he's been here since September," I said. I turned to the other students. "Right?"

All I got was strange looks and more laughter. That and a spitball that came perilously close to my mouth, which was hanging open in amazement.

Ms. Spector held her gaze on me. "There is no Dave Anders on the list," she said again, slowly and deliberately like she was speaking to a small child.

I honestly didn't know how to respond to that. What the heck was going on? Either Ms. Spector was pranking me and had involved the rest of the class, including Dave Anders, or…

Or I'd lost my mind.

I poked my head over her shoulder to stare at the list of names on the clipboard in her hand.

I knew I wasn't crazy, but neither was Ms. Spector.

I scanned the first few names on the list. Allison Andrews. Theo Akhigbe. Tyrone Brown. No Dave Anders.

Had he moved schools and not told anyone?

It was the only explanation that made sense. But why keep it a secret? And why did Ms. Spector have to treat me like some kind of idiot?

Come to think of it, why would the rest of the kids in my class be in on the whole thing too?

I stared at the sea of faces around me. Clearly, I was thinking about this too hard. I lowered my head, picked up a pencil and started doodling zombies and weird alien dudes in my notebook, hoping my classmates would all move on to other things.

A couple of days later I was cutting across the park on the way home from school when I spotted Dave Anders. He hadn't been back to school. In fact, I'd almost forgotten about him altogether, like I had gotten used to the fact that he'd been taken off the attendance list.

Dave was sitting on a park bench, holding a skateboard in his hand and staring at a pile of clothes on the bench beside him.

"Dave!" I called out. "What's going on? Where you have been?"

I marched over to the bench and pushed the pile of clothes aside. They didn't look like Dave's clothes. They looked like they belonged to a much smaller boy.

Dave kept staring at the clothes. He opened his mouth to speak, but no sound came. So I kept talking.

"Hey, it's me, Dave Ziegler. What's going on? Did you change schools? You're not on the class list, and everyone's being weird about it."

Finally Dave looked at me. His hair was a mess. He had dark circles under his eyes, like he'd been awake for days. He was breathing funny, too, as if he'd just finished a long race. And then he spoke, his tone very serious.

"It's not Dave anymore."

"What?"

"You can call me Mike now."

I shook my head. "What are you talking about?"

Dave grabbed me by the shoulder. He leaned in close and then whispered, with great urgency, "You've still got time, I think."

"Huh?"

He gave me another long look. "You haven't noticed it yet, have you?"

"I don't know what the heck you're talking about, Dave—"

"I told you. I'm *Mike* now. You should do the same."

"Do what?"

"Change your name. But you can't just *call* yourself something else. You've got to make it *legal*."

Dave, I mean "Mike," looked over his shoulder, scanning the park like he was worried we were being watched.

I didn't see anything out of the ordinary. There were kids hanging off monkey bars, some adults walking their dogs, and a group of teenagers pushing each other around and laughing.

"Mike" whispered in my ear. "It's moving alphabetically."

"What is?"

"I can't tell you anything more. If you haven't noticed it yet, you will soon."

"Notice what?" I stammered.

"Mike" looked genuinely terrified of something. Terrified enough to quit school and change his name. But whatever it was, why couldn't he tell me? And what did he mean, *alphabetically*?

"David?" a motherly voice called out.

I turned, thinking it might be my mom. But no. It was a woman of about my mom's age, walking through the park with purpose. She was near the playground, searching the horizon. She approached a couple of the adults. Her hands waved wildly as she spoke.

She walked past us, her face lined with worry. "David?" she called out again. Then she suddenly stopped.

She turned to us and froze. She was clearly terrified. But she wasn't looking at either of us.

She was staring at the pile of clothes. Then her mouth dropped open, and her lower lip began to quiver like she was trying to make a sound, or a scream even, but instead this low, raspy noise escaped her throat.

She dropped to her knees, reaching out to grab the shirt on the top of the pile of clothes. She clutched it to her chest, and then she began to panic. "Did you see him?" she asked me.

I just shrugged. "Are those his clothes?" I asked.

Dave Anders had also been freaked out by the pile of clothes. I turned to ask him if knew anything, only to find that he had left, taking his skateboard with him. He hadn't even said goodbye.

He'd really seemed spooked. Did he honestly believe that having the name Dave was some kind of curse?

I thought about it for a minute. What if Dave Anders wasn't crazy, and what he was saying, although it seemed ridiculous, was actually true? Wouldn't there be some kind of evidence somewhere that something was happening to the Daves of the world?

Determined to solve the mystery, I did what anyone would have done. I went home and got on the internet.

I typed *David* into the search engine. I expected I would get hits for all the famous Davids in history. There was that guy from the Bible, the one who fought Goliath and won. And that famous marble statue by Michelangelo we learned about in art class. Or that guy—

I blinked at the words on the screen.

There was nothing on a boy fighting a giant with a slingshot. No naked statue. Nothing.

The word *David* didn't even appear to be recognized on the search string. A line of text asked me, *Did you mean dove?* Below it was a list of suggested websites and a series of pictures of white birds.

"No, not *dove*. Dave!" I couldn't believe I was screaming at a machine.

I opened another search engine and typed in the word *David* again.

Nothing but pictures of white birds. Dove. Dove. Dove.

I felt sweat begin to bead on my forehead and the back of my neck. Maybe it was all in how you phrased your search. I typed in the words *Michelangelo* and *statue*. Surely that would get me at least a picture of the famous sculpture.

"Aha!"

There it was. I knew this had all been a mistake. Or maybe even just a weird hoax, like—

I leaned in closer.

The text under the picture of the famous Italian marble dude with his junk hanging out read **Michelangelo's Bob**.

I was starting to think that maybe I shouldn't be trusting the internet.

I looked over at my bookshelf and the huge set of encyclopedia my grandma had given me. I didn't know the last time I had even looked at them, but I pulled out the volume marked **M** and flipped through the pages to find the entry for Michelangelo. As I expected, there was a picture of the famous sculpture next to his name.

No!

Michelangelo's **Bob**.

There it was! But this encyclopedia had been sitting on my shelf for years!

Whatever was happening to the Daves had gone beyond the internet. But why was only I noticing it? Was it because I was also a Dave? Did I and the other Daves have some strange power now?

"I didn't know you were interested in art," said someone behind me.

I nearly jumped out of my seat. I whirled around. "Mom!" I snapped. "Don't sneak up on me like that."

"Sorry, I just wanted to let you know it's time for dinner, that's all. Why are you looking at the **Bob**?"

I wrinkled my brow. "The what?"

"Michelangelo's **Bob**. Is that for a school project?"

"Mom, it's the **David**. It's always been the **David**."

My mom stopped. She tilted her head to one side and narrowed her eyes, like she was thinking really hard about what I had said. I could see her hands and arms tense. "I think it's always been the **Bob**," she said, in a tone that suggested either I was making a joke or was completely out of the loop.

I began to breathe heavily and in quick bursts.

"It's all right, honey," she said, putting her arm on my shoulder. "It's only a work of art."

I needed to get to the bottom of this Dave situation, and fast. The next day I made a plan to seek out some real people named David. But as it turned out, I didn't know any. Or did I? Had they also dropped off the face of the planet?

Surely there had to be others.

And the best way to find out?

I picked up the phone and dialed the operator.

"Directory assistance, how can I help you?" said a mechanical-sounding voice.

I paused, thinking about where to start.

"Hello? How can I help you?" the operator repeated.

"I'd like the number for…" I paused, remembering what Dave Anders had said about the phenomenon moving alphabetically. I made up a name on the spot. "David Morris."

There was a pause. "I'm sorry. I don't have anyone by that name," said the operator.

I tried again. "How about David Price?"

Another pause. "I'm sorry, sir."

I blurted out the most common surname I could think of. "How about David Smith? I've been trying to reach him for ages!"

"If you are trying to be funny and waste my time, young man, I will end this call right now."

"But..." I started. "Hasn't anyone *else* been looking for these people?"

Maybe my earlier hunch had been correct. Maybe nobody but us Davids knew about what was going on.

I had to know how far this curse had gone. "David Thompson," I said at last.

"Which one?"

"Huh?"

"There are three David Thompsons in this district. Is there one in particular you want to contact?"

"Uh, not right now. I have to run. But thanks!" I hung up the phone.

So the letter *T* was still safe. But how much longer until the curse reached the Zs?

I realized I was a believer now. I didn't know how, or why, but Dave Anders was right. The Davids of the world were disappearing, and fast.

You can't just call *yourself something else. You've got to make it* legal.

That's what Dave had said in the park. Is that how he'd managed to escape whatever this was?

How much time did I have left? I got on the computer and quickly looked up how to change a name. There was a government office in a plaza downtown that provided that service.

I ran out the door and grabbed my bike. I only hoped it wasn't already closed for the day.

I rounded a corner, and cripes—

"David!"

It was my dad, walking home from work. I swerved to avoid slamming right into him. Then I squeezed the brakes and jammed my feet onto the sidewalk to keep from tipping over.

My dad doubled back and put his hand on my shoulder to steady me. "David, what's the matter? Where are you going in such a hurry? It's almost dinnertime."

David. The name made tears well up.

"David, what's wrong?"

"I need to change my name," I said, and I could feel my voice cracking. "All the Daves are disappearing! It's happening faster than I thought, but I can do this. I can fix it."

I could tell from the look on his face that he thought I was crazy.

"I'll explain everything soon. Really soon," I said. Then I added, "I love you, Dad." He looked shocked. I turned and pedaled away as quickly as I could.

I sped up the hill, zipping around corners and cutting across parking lots.

I pedaled past a bus stop and noticed another pile of clothes, crumpled in a heap. I thought I could hear a cell phone ringing.

I gulped.

Had that been another Dave who had vanished into thin air? Zapped by some alien force?

I tried not to think about it as I raced to the plaza.

By the time I pulled my bike into the parking lot, the final rays of the day's sunshine were already hitting the windows and tinting the sky a fiery orange.

I snaked my bike in behind a car pulling in. I hopped the curb and chained my bike beside a newspaper box.

I noticed a man getting out of the parked car. I took a step off the curb toward the office, tripped on something and fell down hard.

The blow from the pavement took the wind out of me, and I desperately heaved air back into my lungs.

Slowly I pushed myself off the ground and looked at my hands. My palms were cut in a few places from some loose rocks on the ground.

Then I noticed the pile of clothes. It was just sitting there, next to the open door of the car.

A complete outfit—shoes, pants, shirt and jacket.

I stared down at it, feeling a sinking sensation in my stomach. Just like at the park. And the bus station.

Clothes, but no body to hold them up.

The man wearing them had been there a moment earlier. I hadn't even heard him scream. He'd been standing there, and now he was gone. There was no trace left of his body. No gory smear on the road or even a smoking heap of remains. No sign that this man had ever existed!

I wondered if the clothes were now clean—because if this Dave had gone, then so would have his dandruff, his flaking skin and any lingering odors or smells that announced his presence in our world.

I almost laughed at this idea, but it was true, wasn't it? I felt sick.

I backed away from the pile of clothes and marched quickly into the office.

I wasn't sure how to go about changing my name, but maybe someone at the front desk would help. There were a few people in line ahead of me. Only one station was open, and the older lady with glasses as thick **as** bulletproof glass didn't seem to be in any hurry.

I watched her helping the man at the counter. He was shifting his weight from foot to foot and checking the clock on the wall. I followed his gaze. It was 4:49. There was no way this office was open past five.

"You must be a **Z**. Maybe a **Y**."

An older man was directly ahead of me in the line. He was wearing a dirty jacket and torn pants. His face was flecked with white stubble. It looked like hadn't changed or shaved or even bathed in a while.

Was he talking to me?

The man nodded. "I had a friend. Dave Walters. But I bet you can guess what happened to him."

I opened my mouth to speak, but no sound came. Dave Walters probably hadn't had time to do what we were both trying to do now.

The old man looked at me with fear in his eyes. "You're so young. Not me, although that's my name. David Young. I'm seventy-eight."

"I'm twelve," I said. I couldn't think of anything else to say.

Wait. That wasn't true. I **did** have a burning question. "What do you think is causing all this?"

David Young rolled his eyes. He licked his dry lips. "At first I thought people were behind it. The government, maybe."

"Why?"

"There are over six billion people on the planet. Not enough resources to keep everyone fit, healthy, alive. So maybe someone came up with a kind of mass hypnosis, maybe using the media, to slowly erase every David from existence. They'd have the name and location of every Dave or David on record."

I didn't know *what* to say to that. "I'm David Ziegler," I said instead.

The old man nodded. "Just like I thought. You're a **Z**."

"Next," the woman called.

I shook my head. "B-but it can't be p-people behind this," I stammered.

The man shrugged. Then he pointed up at the ceiling. "I suppose it could be them," he said.

"Them?"

He leaned in so close to me, I could feel his hot breath in my ear. "Aliens," he whispered. "Real Area 51-type stuff."

Then he leaned back and nodded at me knowingly.

"*Next*," the voice called out again.

Dave Young and I turned and realized that we were already at the front of the line.

"You go on ahead of me."

I looked at him.

"You're young, Dave Ziegler. And if this thing catches up to us, you've still got a lot of life left in you. Me? Like I said, I'm seventy-eight. I've lived a good life."

We were short on time, so I didn't argue.

The woman looked at me and said, "Too young for a driver's license, too young to get married. Let me guess. You're here to change your name." She sounded annoyed.

I nodded.

"But you haven't filled out the forms."

"Oh," I said. **What forms?**

"And you probably didn't bring any identification either, did you?"

I dug my hand into my pocket. I'd raced over here in such a hurry that I'd forgotten to bring my wallet.

Then I heard a sigh and a crunch. The woman at the counter was staring past me, her mouth hanging open.

I turned around.

Dave Young was nowhere to be seen.

I looked at the floor. Where the man Dave Young had been standing only moments before was a pile of clothes. Crumpled shirt. Underwear poking out of pants. Socks still in shoes. Even a pair of horn-rimmed eyeglasses.

Then, without warning, someone stepped on the pile of clothing. I gasped.

"*There* you are. What is going on?" My father looked worried and angry and relieved, all at the same time.

"Dad, I need to change my name. It's the only way to stop it."

"That is enough, David," he snapped. Did he even notice he was stepping on the clothes of a dead man? That is, if you could call *it* death.

Before I could argue, my dad reached out to take my arm.

He clasped his hand around my arm, but the entire sleeve of my shirt began to collapse in on itself.

I started to gasp but couldn't take in any air.

Then I heard the gasp, only it wasn't coming from me. It was coming from my dad. He had a look of shock on his face, which was quickly shifting to horror. He knew! I'd been right all along! This thing, whatever it was, had gone from *A* to *Z*, and that meant I was—

STUFFING

Since they both lived out in the country, Jerome and Marty had a lot of time to kill on the long bus ride home from school. They usually spent it tearing open the back of one of the seats, ripping out the stuffing and throwing it at each other.

They usually got away with it, too, because (a) there were so many other kids doing other crazy things on the bus, and (b) they always sat way at the back.

But on this Tuesday, the driver noticed them.

"Cut that out!" she growled.

Jerome peered down the narrow aisle to the oversized mirror tacked to the ceiling of the bus. His eyes met the driver's. "I think she means us," he said quietly.

"But we're having so much fun." Marty ran his fingers along the back of the seat. It was made of thick green vinyl. And probably covered with the spit and snot of the five million other kids who had been on this ancient bus before them.

Marty got back to work. There was already a sizable tear in the back of the seat. Marty stuck his fingers in and pulled out a hunk of spongy stuffing the size of a golf ball. He waited for the bus driver to start yelling at some other kids, then hurled the hunk at Jerome. It landed right in his mouth.

Jerome screamed, pitched forward and nearly fell into the aisle. There was a loud squeal of grinding metal as the driver slammed on the brakes. This sent twenty or so other kids flying into the backs of the padded seats. Well, mostly padded. Some of them didn't have all of their original stuffing.

"I said, CUT THAT OUT!"

This was not unusual. The bus driver screamed and slammed on the brakes at least three or four times on the runs to and from school, causing about six nosebleeds per week.

Nobody knew the bus driver's name. Jerome wondered if she even had one. He only referred to her as Ms. Grumpy-Butt, which fit her perfectly. She had probably been grown in a lab, as she more closely resembled a lump of flesh that had had stubby limbs and eyes stuck to it than a human. Grumpy-Butt kind of morphed into the same form as the driver's seat. The boys had never seen her get out of it.

By this time the rest of the kids on the bus had swiveled their heads to face Jerome and Marty.

The bus driver glared at them through the mirror. "Stop ripping that stuffing out. Repairing those seats costs money."

She said this as if Jerome or Marty paid taxes or even cared about them. Then she hit the gas pedal with such a fury that everyone on the bus was sent flying again. Behind them, Jerome could see the skid marks the bus tires left on the road.

"I wonder if Grumpy-Butt pays taxes," he whispered to Marty.

"Probably ugly taxes." Marty giggled.

"Keep your feet on the floor," the bus driver said to the kids, "and sit up straight."

Jerome and Marty were the last two to get off the bus. The ride home for them took about half an hour with all the stops, chugging along country roads that seemed to stretch into infinity.

Marty got off first. For the last five minutes of the drive, Jerome usually moved up to sit near Grumpy-Butt. Not right beside her, but close enough that he could hop off the bus when it was his turn.

Today, as they neared Marty's house, Jerome followed his friend to the front of the bus.

The driver ground the bus to a halt.

Marty started to make his way off the bus, but Grumpy-Butt flung out her arm and caught him across the stomach. Marty gasped for breath.

"You're going to pay for that stuffing you tore out," Grumpy-Butt said.

"Huh?" Marty turned to face the driver.

She stared out the front window. "You heard me."

"Who cares?" Marty said. "It's only stuffing. Why don't you just do your job and drive us to and from school?" He turned and stormed down the steps.

The door slammed shut in his face before he could exit the vehicle.

"Ouch! What did you do that for?"

"Apologize."

"What?"

"I said, *apologize.*" Ms. Grumpy-Butt finally turned her head and leered at him. Her fake-red curls bounced.

"No way. Let me out. Or I'll...I'll get my parents to *sue* you." Marty's dad was a lawyer, and Marty often used this threat when he had run out of smart things to say.

"Let it go," said Jerome. He knew Marty, and from what he knew of Grumpy-Butt, neither of them was the type to back down from an argument.

"Seriously? You're on her side?"

"I want to go home," Jerome said.

"Fine. I apologize. I'm sorry!" Marty roared.

He stared at the driver. The driver stared back at him. Jerome watched as the two of them narrowed their eyes until they were slits.

Then the driver threw her head back and let out a throaty laugh. She opened the door.

"I'm sorry you're such a loser!" Marty spat out as he flung himself off the bus. He ran toward his house without even glancing back.

Jerome sunk into his seat. He got up the nerve to look in the rearview mirror and saw that the driver was staring right at him with her beady little eyes.

Jerome quickly glanced out the window and counted the seconds until his stop.

Jerome couldn't figure out where Marty was the next day. He always got picked up first on the ride to school. But he was not on the bus when Jerome climbed on.

"Is Marty okay?" Jerome asked the driver as they snaked down the dirt road to the next stop.

The driver mumbled something, but Jerome didn't catch it. He didn't know why he'd asked her anyway. The bus came to an abrupt halt. A wave of five or six kids started to climb aboard. Jerome waddled down to his usual seat at the back. It felt weird without Marty there. And weird that he hadn't texted him or anything.

Without his sidekick, Jerome had nothing to do, so he just stared out the window for the entire boring ride to school.

Marty didn't show up at school late either. Jerome figured maybe he had a doctor's appointment or something. That meant there would be no one to have a stuffing fight with on the bus ride home.

Jerome hopped on and stared out the dirty window. He occupied himself thinking about the scary movies he wanted to download when he got home. The bus cleared town and rattled down the dusty country roads.

The area where he and Marty lived, outside the main town, would be a great place to shoot a horror movie, Jerome decided. It was so remote, and the houses were so far apart. He imagined scenes with creatures stalking people through the woods or tall grasses, or along the vast farmers' fields, on cold gray afternoons like this one.

"Mrrrmph."

The sound caught Jerome's attention and brought him back to the bus. He'd been daydreaming for so long, lost in his thoughts, that he'd completely missed all the other kids getting off. He was the only one left on the bus.

He looked at the back of the seat in front of him. The padding looked strangely lumpy. Jerome wondered if Ms. Grumpy-Butt or someone at the school office had thrown in some new kind of padding to replace the stuffing he and Marty had pulled out.

They had done a pretty crappy job. The tear he and Marty had made had been resealed with black hockey tape. Jerome picked at the stretchy tape, which left dark smudges on his fingers. Once he started, it was impossible to stop. He peeled a few strips of the tape back and stretched open the tear.

The stuffing inside was in loose bits. Jerome squeezed some between his fingers and pulled a chunk out.

He was about to stuff the chunk back, thinking he'd better not make Grumpy-Butt mad again, when he noticed the hair.

There were several strands. More like a clump, really. Jerome figured it was probably Ms. Grumpy-Butt's, but then he looked closer. No. Her hair was red and curly, while this clump was straight and brown. Jerome pulled on it.

The seat let out a yelp.

Jerome jerked back. He swallowed, but all the spit in his mouth had suddenly dried up. He glanced above the top of the seat. The driver had her eyes on the road.

Jerome leaned in closer and tugged on the hockey tape. The tear in the seat opened a little bit more. Just enough for Jerome to reach his hand in. He pulled out another clump of stuffing.

His stomach did three somersaults. He could see now that the hair was attached to a head.

A human head. Inside the bus seat.

Jerome jammed his fist into his mouth and bit down on it. He wanted to scream, *tried* to scream. The only sound that escaped his lips was a strangled whisper.

The head turned his way. A single eye peered out through the rip in the seat.

The bus braked suddenly. Jerome pitched forward, slamming into the seat. The body in the seat gave another pained cry.

Marty's cry!

Jerome pulled his face away from the seat and looked out the window. He realized they should have reached his stop by now. Instead, the bus had pulled over to the side of a small road Jerome didn't recognize. The landscape was flecked with twisted shrubs and hills. There was no sign of any houses. Jerome looked over his shoulder and through the window in the emergency exit at the back. No cars were heading this way either.

Jerome stood up. He wanted to help Marty, he really did. But his instincts were telling him to run. **Now.** Jerome tried the emergency handle on the rear door, but it wouldn't budge.

"You're the *other* one who's been tearing out all the stuffing," said the driver.

Jerome slowly turned around. Ms. Grumpy-Butt was still squashed into her seat, but he could see her reflection in the rearview mirror. There was a sinister gleam in her eye.

"I'm sorry. Really, really sorr—"

"Throwing it around the bus like it's popcorn or something."

"Please," Jerome begged. "It won't happen again. I won't—"

"And that stuffing costs money. Do I look like I'm rolling in dough?"

"No," Jerome managed. "But I can pay for this."

"Exactly," Ms. Grumpy-Butt said, getting out of her seat. Jerome noticed she had something in her hands. A thick roll of black hockey tape, the kind she patched the seats with. She pulled off a big strip. "You'll definitely be paying for those seats."

Jerome dug into his pockets. He only had a couple of dollars in change on him. But he had more. A whole bank account full of money! However much she needed...

"And as you can see," the bus driver cooed, "I have a lot of seats to fill."

THE READING GROUP

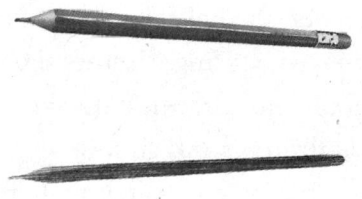

Mr. Wexler could disguise it all he wanted to. He could call it Group 1, or Red Group, or even "Wexler's Buddies," which he'd tried. *Once.* But Maya knew what everyone really called it. The dumb group. The can't-read group. The never-get-good-grades group. The losers.

It was just Andrew Kim, Noah Lazar and Maya. Even among the no-gooders, she was the only girl. Every other reading group had at least four people. The high group had six people in it—and Maya knew it was the high group because every one in it got straight As. Madeleine Beltzner made sure to let everyone know that every time they got a test back.

An A! Again! she would always shout, waving her test like it was a golden ticket. Mr. Wexler only worked with the high group once in a while, because they didn't need to be taught.

Not Maya. Apparently, she'd needed one-on-one time with every teacher she'd had since kindergarten. She didn't mind the extra help. What she couldn't stand was the way everyone looked at her, like she was some kind of broken thing.

One day Mr. Wexler sat Maya down and asked her to read a booklet about flowers and bees.

Flowers and bees were okay, but Maya couldn't focus on the words, even when she held the booklet close to her face. Even when she moved her finger across the words. They just looked like symbols, not even letters she could recognize. Sticks and lines and curves and circles.

She knew Mr. Wexler was watching her every move. He was timing how fast she read, scribbling notes in his pad. The longer she took to decode a word, the faster his pen scratched against the paper. The faster the pen scratched, the more she could hear the Sound.

It was a sound that was only in her head. Maya often heard it when she tried to concentrate really hard on something, like doing well on a reading test. It was a low drone, almost as if a bumblebee was hovering just beyond her ear. The Sound had been with her ever since she was a little girl, but it seemed to be growing louder and louder these days.

Maya concentrated on the booklet Mr. Wexler wanted her to read. She tried sounding out the words, moving her mouth and lips to form what she hoped was written on the page, but the Sound was louder than she'd ever heard it before.

Forget the buzz of one bumblebee going on inside her head—it was like a whole hive of them!

Suddenly Mr. Wexler pulled the booklet away from Maya, catching her off guard. She gasped and then realized Mr. Wexler was saying something.

She rubbed the sides of her head. That seemed to make the Sound fade. It was still there, but now it was only a dull murmur nipping at the back of her mind. Mr. Wexler spoke again. "You can stop now, Maya."

Maya glanced over her shoulder. The rest of the class was supposed to be doing quiet reading, but most of them were looking at her with wide eyes and open mouths. Had she screamed? Said something stupid?

"Are you okay, Maya?" Mr. Wexler asked, trying to catch her attention.

Maya turned back to him. Her face went red. She felt hot. She nodded.

Mr. Wexler stared at her. He opened his mouth like he wanted to say something else, but stopped himself. He waited for the other students to stop staring. Then he reached down to the suitcase by his feet and fished out a piece of paper. He handed it to Maya.

It was more like a piece of cardboard than paper. It was laminated too. Maya could see a clear border around it, as well as fingerprints from other kids who had obviously used it before her. Maya tried to focus on the words on it. The letters were much larger than she was used to seeing in books. They were the size of letters in books for little babies. She narrowed her eyes. "What's this?"

"It's something I think you should read," Mr. Wexler said. His voice was quiet. Almost a whisper. He motioned to the study corner. There was a desk set up there with a barrier wall so you could work privately. Usually Mr. Wexler sent the troublemakers over there so they wouldn't disturb the rest of the class.

"I want to go back to my desk," Maya said.

Mr. Wexler shook his head. "I'd like you to go read this over there," he said firmly. "And take your pencil with you."

Maya didn't want to make Mr. Wexler angry, and he was using the tone he saved for the kids who liked to push his buttons. Still, a pencil? "Is it a test?" Maya asked.

"Go read it and find out."

Maya didn't say anything else. She got up from the horseshoe-shaped table she'd been sitting at and walked over to the study corner. The rickety desk was covered with graffiti and had all sorts of bad words carved into it with staples and unfolded paper clips.

Maya pulled the chair out, sat down and looked at the paper. She had to blink a few times before the words came into focus.

As they did, the Sound came swimming back into her head. Only this time the Sound didn't make the words look wrong. The Sound seemed to help now, working almost like a pair of glasses.

The letters were so big that they took up most of the page. *MAKE THE PENCIL FLOAT.*

Maya blinked. That's what it said.

She looked over at Mr. Wexler, hoping for some kind of explanation. But he was sitting at the horseshoe-shaped table with another group of students. Maya turned back to the paper. The buzzing in her head was growing louder. It was almost a kind of itch, and the only way she could scratch it was to—

The pencil.

She focused on her pencil lying on the desk. The Sound buzzed in her head. She traced the outline of the pencil in her mind, like she was taking a mental picture of it. But her mental picture was so real that she could almost feel it. Like she could touch it. Not with her hands, but with her thoughts.

The pencil wobbled.

Maya gasped. She looked over her shoulder. Mr. Wexler was still busy with that group of kids. He hadn't seen. She glanced over the barrier and scanned the class. Nobody else had seen either. She was sure of it.

She looked back at the pencil. Her heart was racing. She swallowed, stared at the pencil and heard the Sound. It washed over her like a cold ocean wave. She trained her mind on the pencil again.

The pencil rolled toward her hand.

Maya made it stop just before it touched her pinky.

She glanced at the words on the page again.

MAKE THE PENCIL FLOAT.

Why not?

She was still tracing the pencil with her thoughts. Now all she had to do was think, *Float*. The pencil wobbled and then, very gently, very slowly, lifted into the air.

Maya leaned in close to make sure no one else could see the floating pencil. It was only a few inches off the desk. She held it there for a minute, and then let go.

The Sound died away. It was still there, nibbling at her thoughts, but she didn't mind it as much.

When Mr. Wexler had finished with the kids at the horseshoe table, Maya brought the paper over to him, still not sure how to explain what had happened. Mr. Wexler spoke first. "Did you enjoy the text?"

"I... I..."

"I can see you are making excellent progress so far." He didn't smile, but somehow Maya got the feeling Mr. Wexler was very, very pleased.

He took the paper from Maya's hand and put it back into his suitcase. Maya caught a glimpse of other papers in the suitcase, all neatly arranged. She had the feeling Mr. Wexler wanted her to see all the papers, but then the bell rang, and the other kids rushed out of the classroom.

"Have a good recess," Mr. Wexler said without looking at her.

He didn't mention the pencil or the paper for the rest of the day.

Maya tried lifting the pencil again when she got home from school.

She didn't need to read the words on the paper. It wasn't just because she'd memorized them. It was something about the way the words had appeared. Up until now the Sound in her head had been locked up, but the paper had acted like some kind of key.

It was easy to lift the pencil—and other objects too. She tried an eraser and then a piece of paper. It was tricky at first, but she got the hang of it quickly enough.

After a few hours of practice, Maya was able to lift the paper into the air, write her name on it in pencil and then erase it. She kept all three things in the air with her mind, like a juggler using their hands.

There was a knock at the bedroom door.

All three objects fell to the floor.

The door opened. It was her father, home from work. He frowned. "Didn't you hear me knocking? I've been calling you for dinner for five minutes."

Maya nodded vacantly. "Oh."

"Are you okay?"

Maya stared into her father's eyes. Was her special talent genetic? Did her father or mother have the same ability? Did other people?

Maya could tell her dad had no idea his daughter could make pencils float in the air. She wasn't sure how, but she knew. Just as she was certain that Mr. Wexler had picked up on her "talent" earlier that day.

She decided not to tell her father or her mother about the pencil.

The next day Mr. Wexler called Maya's reading group to the horseshoe table at the beginning of class.

He set one pencil down in front of the three of them. He did not give any of them sheets of paper to write on or any other pencils.

"Go on, Maya," Mr. Wexler said. "Show us what you learned yesterday."

Andrew and Noah stared at Maya. She focused the Sound, traced a thought bubble around the pencil and rolled it toward Andrew without even looking at it.

The pencil rolled so fast that Andrew had to snap his hand against the desk to keep it from falling off.

"I see you did some homework," said Mr. Wexler.

He opened the briefcase by his feet and fished out three more pieces of laminated paper, all identical. Maya stared at the words on the page: **TURN THE LIGHTS ON AND OFF.**

Immediately the lights above her head flickered off. Maya shot a glance over to Noah and saw a big grin spreading across his face. A second later the lights flicked back on, and Maya turned to see Andrew with the same smile on his face, nodding.

"What's going on?" someone said.

Maya turned and saw a few of her classmates staring up at the lights.

"I'm sure it's just a power surge," Mr. Wexler said, raising his voice so the others could hear. "Nothing to worry about. Everyone back to your desks, please."

The lights flicked on and off a couple more times. Maya noticed that Mr. Wexler was staring at her intently. "Well?"

Maya tilted her head to look up at the fluorescent bulbs overhead. At first she thought about wrapping her thoughts around the light switches and flicking them on and off. But what if the other kids saw the switches moving? They'd freak out.

No, there had to be a better way. Using her mind, she traced lines around the long tubular bulbs themselves. She could feel the gases inside. She squeezed her thoughts around the slender bulbs, pushing at the gases, coaxing them—

The lights blazed to brilliant life, as if someone had stuck flares inside the tubes.

Around her, Maya heard screams.

She gasped, feeling the crackle of electricity in her head, and let go.

The lights faded.

Mr. Wexler got out of his chair, flicked the lights on, off and then on again. He stared at them with a puzzled look on his face, obviously putting on a show for the class. "Just what I thought," he said loudly. "A power surge." He gave the briefest of glances at Maya.

Then Mr. Wexler sat himself back down at the horseshoe table. He took back the three pieces of laminated paper and pulled out another set. He passed one to each of the students.

Maya noticed that hers was not laminated. It was a plain piece of paper with the word **TEST** handwritten on it.

"Huh?" Maya asked. "You want us to do a reading test?"

Why do you need to read words, Maya, when you can read minds?

Only then did Maya notice that Mr. Wexler's lips were not moving. She could hear his voice in her head.

I've been waiting for this moment, Maya. I've been watching you ever since kindergarten, because you're one of us. Mr. Wexler's thoughts were beaming right into her head.

One of us? Maya asked, only her mouth didn't move. But Mr. Wexler could hear her just fine.

There aren't many of us around, Maya. Because we're special. We have a gift.

A gift, another voice echoed. It slithered around her mind, trying to probe its way in. Maya turned to see Noah smiling at her in a way that set her hairs on end.

"Read the paper," Mr. Wexler said.

"I did read it," Maya said.

"You looked at the word, but you didn't read it," Mr. Wexler continued. As he talked, Maya realized there were other words being said, only those words were traveling directly from Mr. Wexler's head into her own. *The test isn't this paper, Maya. It's the people behind you, sitting in their desks.*

Maya turned.

"Read the letters on the paper carefully. Sound them out one by one," Mr. Wexler said out loud. But in his mind he added, *Choose one of them. Use your gift, Maya, and dig into their thoughts.*

"T-Est," Maya sounded out.

"Again," Mr. Wexler said, but in her mind, Maya heard, *Why not Madeleine?*

"T-Est."

Mr. Wexler's voice entered her mind. *I know how you feel about her. The way she looks at you like you're a piece of trash. I can hear what she says, too, and it isn't very nice.*

You didn't have to be a mind reader to know what Madeleine Beltzner and her friends said about Maya. It wasn't anything new.

But even thinking about the things Madeleine whispered about her made the back of Maya's neck itch and her ears get hot. Maya looked down and noticed that her hands were clenched into tight fists.

They torment you, don't they?

They do, Maya heard Andrew and Noah think together. Had Mr. Wexler been saying other things into Andrew's and Noah's minds? Things Maya couldn't hear but they could?

They make fun of you. They've always *made fun of you. Yes, they do!*

The voices battered around Maya's head.

They do not know the powers we possess, thought Mr. Wexler.

Maya's heart began to beat faster. She could hear the horrible things that were brewing in Andrew's deepest, darkest thoughts. His head was full of thoughts of revenge for all the times kids had picked on him. He was thinking about picking students up as easily as Maya had the pencil. Thinking about sending Madeleine Beltzner flying across a room. Maya thought about how Madeleine would look, the horror on her face. She pictured her in the air, coming closer and closer to the wall, and—

No! Maya thought privately.

But there weren't any private thoughts between the members of the reading group.

No? Mr. Wexler repeated.

You can't hurt them, Maya thought.

Who said we were going to hurt them?

I saw what Andrew was planning.

What did you see?

Maya tried to bury her thoughts deep within her. She turned up the Sound in her mind. It buzzed and whirred like a dryer or washing machine, making white noise. She turned the Sound up loud enough that Andrew, Noah and even Mr. Wexler could not hear her.

What are you thinking, Maya?

She does not agree with us, thought Andrew.

Not with our plan.

Their thoughts swarmed around her brain like angry hornets. Their voices were growing more and more angry. They stung at the layers of her brain, trying to get into her thoughts. Maya bit down on her lip so hard that she tasted blood.

Mr. Wexler's thoughts surged above the others. *Do you think I invited you into this reading group to help the other students? They are beneath us, Maya.*

Beneath us! Andrew or Noah echoed. Or maybe it was both of them.

There are others out there like us. Can't you hear them?

Maya could hear other thoughts. They were distant, to be sure, but they washed back and forth across the back of her mind like waves at some far-off beach.

It begins today. It begins now, thought Mr. Wexler.

Maya was suddenly aware that the horseshoe table had begun to vibrate. She cast quick glances at Andrew, Noah and Mr. Wexler. Their palms were pressed against the table. Their eyes were rolled back in their sockets. Their jaws hung slack, and their tongues were rolling out of their open mouths like tentacles.

She looked over her shoulder. The entire class was staring at them.

"Mr. Wexler...?"

The horseshoe table kept vibrating. It made a low tone like the Sound in Maya's head. The vibrating was the same Sound—it was *their* sound—and it was making the whole table shudder and rock. The bolts and screws started to pop out of the table, and as it rose a few inches off the floor it began to wobble uncontrollably.

Maya stood up. Mr. Wexler and the other members of her reading group still remained firmly in place, their hands braced against the table.

One or two students were brave enough to take a few tentative steps toward the reading group.

"Don't..." Maya started. Then her mind flared with pain. Mr. Wexler and the boys were stabbing at her head from the inside.

Join us, or them, if you choose, but think about who will win this war.

Maya reached deep into her mind. She could hear other voices swimming through her thoughts. So many of them were full of anger and hate. They were the voices of people who had been laughed at, picked on, cast aside.

But there were other voices too. Voices of people who wanted to take a stand against the Mr. Wexlers of the world. These voices were almost drowned out by the roar of the angry voices, but they were there.

Maya knew what she had to do.

Behind her, Mr. Wexler and the boys were using their powers to pick up the pencils in the room and suspend them in the air. Maya saw their sharpened points, all aimed at her, and gulped.

They wanted to get rid of her. Maya obviously posed some kind of threat to Mr. Wexler, Andrew and Noah. She didn't know what she could do. All she knew was that they had to be stopped. She'd have to do something to startle them, to scare them enough that their minds reeled for a moment.

Maya looked up and saw the lights.

She dropped the cloud she'd wrapped around her mind to protect it from Mr. Wexler. Immediately she could feel Andrew and Noah start to squeeze their thoughts around her, like a python to prey.

Maya cried out but concentrated her thoughts on the lights.

She flexed.

The lights blazed like fires. The bulbs shattered. Glass rained down on the classroom. Students screamed.

The pencils dropped to the floor.

The horseshoe table had slammed back to the floor too. Mr. Wexler and the boys were clutching their heads in pain. The rest of the students began running out of the room, screaming and yelping with fear.

But the reading group wouldn't be in pain for much longer. Mr. Wexler and the boys would get their strength back soon, unless Maya stopped them first.

She focused her mind on the floor. With a quick thought, she scooped up the sharpened pencils and lifted them in the air.

Maya gulped.

She thought very carefully about what she was doing. There were others like her, right now, thinking the same horrible thoughts. Knowing they had no other choice.

Maya closed her eyes, took hold of the pencils, aimed them at the others in group and

Made.

Them.

Move!

EVIL EYE

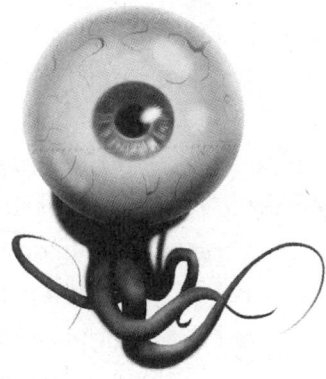

"Can you open your eye for me?" The doctor's voice was calm and soothing. But Jane's eye was burning. It felt like someone had struck a match against it and held it there while the flame lit. She shook her head.

"Jane," the doctor said, "I need to see your eye before we can figure out what's wrong with it—"

"It hurts, that's what's wrong with it!" Jane could barely keep back the tears. She was almost crying because she was scared, but mostly because her eye felt like a volcano.

Jane had been on a school field trip. The whole class had taken a bus to the old cemetery on the edge of town. People rarely visited it because it was so old. There hadn't been a funeral service held there for years. It was overgrown with weeds and half-dead trees, and it stank of rotting things. Jane's class had come to make rubbings of the tombstones.

They were each supposed to get rubbings of the names and dates from at least three tombstones. Then they would search through the library to find information about the dead people. Jane's teacher, Mr. Schmelp, had said it was important for the students to learn some local history. He was a bit strange.

Jane had taken her time in the cemetery. She'd walked past the thorn shrubs to the far end of the graveyard, leaving her class behind. Hiding in the shadows was a crumbling tombstone. The letters had been softened by wind and time, but Jane could make out the inscription: **HERE LIES SHAWN CRUMB**. Mr. Crumb's tombstone was leaning against the rusted iron fence. Jane didn't want to touch it. She was afraid it might fall apart in her hands.

But then she felt the urge.

It was as if the tombstone was calling to her somehow. Jane stepped forward, trying to figure out why she'd singled out this one grave. She closed her eyes, and that's when she noticed the sound, so faint it was at the very edge of her range of hearing. Almost like a whisper. Almost like words, even. But they were too hard to hear. She had to get closer to the tombstone.

Jane took out a piece of paper and a crayon. She leaned forward.

That was when Matteo had pushed her. Matteo always pushed people, especially girls and *especially* Jane.

Jane didn't go face-first into the dirt like Matteo had probably planned. But she did catch her foot, and it twisted as she fell, which caused her head to slap against the grubby tombstone. When Jane hit the ground, she felt her eye start to swell immediately. Mr. Schmelp had called her mom, who'd raced home from work and taken her to the hospital.

Now Jane was sitting on an observation table, on a crinkly paper sheet. The sheet was big enough for at least three tombstone rubbings. But Jane couldn't think about that now.

The doctor shone a light at Jane's face. She clenched her eyelids shut.

"If you open your eye for me, maybe you'll get a lollipop."

How old did he think she was? Jane opened her other eye to see if the doctor was joking.

The doctor forced her bad eye open with his thumb and index finger and shone a light into her eye. Jane clenched her teeth. Her eye felt like it was going to explode out of its socket. If it did, Jane hoped it would explode all over the doctor.

"I thought so," the doctor told Jane's parents, sitting nearby. "She's scratched her cornea."

Scratched cornea? That sounded bad.

The doctor patted her on the back, but Jane didn't feel any better. "You'll be fine," he reassured her. "But I'm going to have to ask you to wear a patch for a day or two."

Then the doctor put some drops into Jane's eye and covered it with enough gauze and tape to make her head look like a mummy's. "I'm sure you'll be right as rain in no time," he said.

He didn't give Jane a lollipop.

"Who the heck is that?"

"I think it's Jane."

"Is she all right?"

"She looks like a pirate." The last voice was Matteo's. He put his hands on his hips, screwed one eye shut and turned to the others. "Arrrrr. We'll make her walk the plank before the bell rings."

"You're such a weirdo, Matteo," Erin told him. Then the bell rang. Matteo pushed Erin onto the pavement and lined up for class.

Mr. Schmelp told the class that they were having a math test. Everyone had to take it except Jane. She wasn't allowed to read while she had the patch on because she might strain her eye. Jane started to think that maybe this whole eye-patch thing wasn't going to be so bad after all.

Plus, she got to watch Matteo write the test.

Matteo had been staring at his paper for over ten minutes.

Jane smiled as she watched Mario look from the clock to his paper. Then he looked back at the clock. He chewed on the end of his pencil. He ran his fingers through his hair. He put his hand up to ask a question. When Mr. Schmelp shook his head, Matteo lowered his hand.

He tried looking over the shoulder of the girl in front of him for the answers, but Mr. Schmelp was still watching him.

Matteo turned around to see Jane smiling. "What are *you* looking at, Long Jane Silver?" he asked. The whole class burst out laughing. Jane wasn't smiling anymore. And her eye started to sting again.

That night Jane had one of those dreams where you can see yourself floating away from your body. For a brief moment she was staring down at herself. Then she turned and floated away through the space under the door.

Jane wasn't too sure how she could fit through that space, but this was a dream, and in dreams you don't worry about the rules. Now Jane was floating down the staircase. Through an open window. And then she was outside.

The darkness cloaked the street like soot in a chimney. Jane felt the chill of the night and wanted to shiver. Most of her dreams happened in flashes. When she woke up, it was hard to remember the details. But this dream was so vivid. She seemed to be floating down the street toward her school.

A pair of headlights emerged at the end of the street. Jane immediately swerved and took shelter behind some nearby bushes until the car drove past. When the red taillights disappeared behind her, Jane came out from behind the bushes and continued to float on. Something was telling her to be cautious. Was it because she was on the street in the middle of the night? Was something stalking her out there in the darkness? Jane felt the chills again, only this time it had less to do with the temperature.

Finally she was at the school. She circled above it like a hawk. The doors were probably locked. The windows were shut—

No. Not all of them. One of the windows was open. Just a sliver. Just enough to let some fresh air in.

Jane felt herself floating forward. There was no way she could fit through that tiny crack! She tried to stop herself from smashing through the glass, but this was a dream...

Now she was in her own classroom, floating past the rows of desks to the heavy table that Mr. Schmelp used as a desk. Right on top was a bundle of papers from that day's math test. All marked.

Jane hovered over the table and stared at the questions. And the answers.

The next morning Jane's mother removed the eye patch. "I see you tried to take it off yourself," she said, picking at a bit of the tape that had come loose.

Jane blinked a few times and looked at herself in the mirror. Her eye seemed as good as new. The skin around her eye was pale and still a bit clammy, but it was nothing that a good scrub with a facecloth couldn't fix. Jane blinked again, looked at her reflection and smiled. She could see again.

Jane was still smiling at breakfast, when she brushed her teeth and when she left for school. A smile was still on her face when she lined up to go inside, when she took her coat off and went to her desk and even when it came time to sing the national anthem.

The smile only faded when Mr. Schmelp came to her desk and handed her some stapled sheets of paper, turned over. "You didn't think I would forget about you," he said.

"Huh?"

"The math test you missed yesterday, of course."

Jane turned over the papers and gulped. It was the test she had seen in her dream.

The *exact* same test.

Jane's eye started to twitch, but she blinked it back under her control. Then a different sort of smile slid across her cheeks. She was going to ace this.

Jane was still smiling when she came home that night, still smiling when she ate her brussels sprouts (much to the confusion of her parents, since she'd always hated brussels sprouts), still smiling when she finished her homework. Then she slipped into her pajamas and went to bed.

Soon sleep overtook her, and Jane found herself in a dark room she didn't recognize. As her vision adjusted, she could make out that it was a bedroom, a messy one, with cluttered shelves and clothes on the floor.

Jane looked at the bed. She recognized the person tangled up in the covers.

Jane woke with a start. She was sweating so much that her pajamas stuck to her skin like wallpaper. She was pretty sure she had just had a nightmare. She got out of bed to get a glass of water.

The boy in the bed was Matteo. She could still see his room in her mind as clear as day. It was so clear she could even count the wrinkles in Matteo's sheets.

Jane filled the cup with water from the tap and gulped it back. The night light was on in the bathroom, so she didn't have to flip the switch on. She looked in the mirror.

Her hair was a mess, her eye was missing—

Jane dropped the cup. It clattered to the floor, water spilling everywhere.

She shut her eye—*eyes!* She shut her *eyes.*

(She could still see Matteo's room.)

Stop thinking about Matteo's room and open your eyes!

Jane opened them. Messy hair, missing eye. Perfect. Perfect. Per—

Why was this so perfect?

Jane realized she must still be dreaming. All she had to do was go back to bed, pull the covers up over her head and sleep until morning. Then everything would be fine. She'd get up and brush her teeth and two eyes would be staring back at her from the bathroom mirror and—

Jane clutched the cold porcelain of the sink.

The picture in her mind—the one of Matteo's room—was changing. She was floating up to the shelves on the wall. She was staring at them hard, like she was looking for something. What was she looking for?

Jane shook the thought from her head. She stared at herself in the bathroom mirror and leaned in close. There was her eye socket, empty as a donut hole. With only the night light on, it was too dim to see anything beyond the darkness of the socket. Jane wondered what would happen if she turned on the bathroom light. Would she be able to see into her brain? She resisted the temptation to stick her finger into the gaping hole in her head. And besides, what would her mom and dad think when they saw her like this? Think of something else, she told herself. Her mind immediately returned to Matteo's room.

Then she saw it. She was hovering near a shelf above Matteo's bed. It was a bookcase. The books were held in place by two heavy bookends, but they were very, very close to the edge of the shelf.

Jane shut her eyelids to see the picture more clearly.

The books were angled against one bookend. She could see that the bookend was half on the shelf, half off. All she had to do was push some of the standing books over. A little nudge would do it. The books would fall like dominoes. The bookend would fall off the shelf—

Matteo's head was directly under the shelf.

Don't even think it! But she already was. That was just it. Jane *was* thinking it. *Push it over. Just a little nudge—*

Jane raced out of the bathroom, thundered downstairs, jammed her feet in her father's boots and ran out into the street.

It didn't take her long to get to Matteo's, but by the time she got there her lungs stung from the cold. She looked around the house for a way in. The windows were shut. The curtains were drawn. The front door was locked. But nailed to the side of the house was a white trellis, overgrown with vines and creepers. Jane shook off her dad's boots and began to climb. When she reached the window, she forced it open with one hand.

Into Matteo's room spilled Jane and the night wind. She tumbled to the carpet and was on her feet in a second. Matteo still lay in his bed, sound asleep.

Jane caught something moving in the corner of her eye.

It was the eye. *Her* eye. She could see herself staring at herself. *Weird!*

For a moment Jane and the eye stared each other off. Matteo still hadn't stirred.

The eye floated toward her. Its pupil contracted to a tiny dot. Somehow the eye looked angry.

Jane backed up until she was against the closet door. She flung it open. Clothes and toys spilled to the floor. Jane reached for the first thing she could find to defend herself with and clasped her palm around it.

The eye saw it too, but it was coming so fast there was no time for it to escape.

Thwack! Jane held a tennis racket in one hand.

The eyeball flew back, hit the far wall with a thud (leaving a gooey splotch) and landed on the floor.

Jane concentrated on the picture in her mind. It was dark. Clutching the racket, she inched her way forward. Still dark. Jane passed the edge of bed and noticed a pile of dirty clothes.

She clutched the racket handle so hard she thought it might snap. She reached with her other hand toward the laundry. She would have to do this. She would have to pick up Matteo's grubby shirt and use it to try to grab the eye.

No. That would be too obvious. The eye would know—

Jane stopped herself. This was ridiculous. She was in a boy's room in the middle of the night, without any shoes, trying to catch her own runaway eye. And he was sleeping through all of it! For all she knew, she was probably still dreaming this all up and—

The eye shot out of the pile and came flying right at her.

Jane swatted at the eye again. Too little, too late. She knew exactly where it was headed. The shelf.

Jane whirled around and dropped the racket.

The eye hit the bookend. The bookend hit the books.

Jane jumped onto Matteo's bed. Matteo's eyes shot open. He started to scream when he caught sight of one-eyed Jane above him.

The books knocked into the other bookend.

With all her strength, Jane pushed Matteo off the bed.

It felt good to push Matteo for once.

Then Jane leaped from the bed, so all the books could crush was a pillow.

Matteo could only look at Jane the cyclops and point in horror. His eyes would not shut, even as the rest of the books spilled to the empty bed behind him. A few papers fluttered down after the books like confetti. Matteo's eyes remained open as a draft from the open window made one of the papers zoom past Jane's head. They would not shut even as the sharp edge of the page slashed across his open eye.

Matteo shrieked and clutched his head with his hands. Just then his bedroom door was flung open. There stood his parents. Before either of them could even blurt out a "What's going on here?" Jane was on the move.

She couldn't see the eye, but in her mind she could see an image of the neighborhood street, so she knew it had somehow escaped. She pushed past Matteo's parents, bounded down the stairs and flung the door open. She stopped on the step for a moment, shuddering. She knew where she had to go.

Jane entered the cemetery, and only then did she realize she'd been running barefoot. Her toes and the balls of her heels sunk into the mud, and she had to wrench her feet out for each step forward. She was going to need a bath when this was all over.

It was impossible to find the eye in the darkness, but Jane could still see what it saw. It did not have an eyelid to shield itself. It could only stare at the leaves on the ground and the deteriorating tombstones. One tombstone in particular. Jane recognized the weathered letters instantly: *HERE LIES SHAWN CRUMB.*

Jane reached the tombstone and saw herself seeing herself from a perspective not too far away. In the moonlight Jane spotted her other eye hovering near a gnarled tree. Jane followed its gaze to the earth in front of the tombstone. She was startled to realize that something was poking through the dirt.

Ten somethings, to be precise. They wiggled their way through the earth like seedlings in a stop-motion film. Jane got down on her knees to regard them more closely. The somethings were white, all right, although they were too thick to be seedlings. But they were growing all the same. Now they were an inch out of the soil. They wiggled at Jane, pushing dirt out of their way so they could sprout farther. Jane moved away. The somethings had fingernails.

She was on her feet and backing up now, but she could not look away from the grave.

Fingernails belonged to fingers. Fingers belonged to hands. They were human hands, but the skin that clung to them had withered and dried into a leathery husk. Some of the skin had torn, revealing yellowing bones underneath. The hands pushed aside the dirt, and then the arms erupted from the earth. Jane put her hand to her mouth and held back the scream.

She thought about running away. It was the logical thing to do when one was confronted with a corpse digging itself out of a grave. Jane had often stayed up late to watch horror movies, and she'd always thought it was amazing how stupid people could be, walking into haunted houses or going near shadowy corners that had weird noises coming from them. Jane figured she had to be at least as stupid as those people in the movies, because there she was, in the middle of the night, in a cemetery, standing mere feet away from the living dead, and she had not moved a muscle.

Jane was still standing there when those skeletal arms pushed aside enough mossy earth for the corpse's head to emerge. Her stomach turned and twisted like a pretzel.

A few strands of hair still clung to the remains of the corpse's scalp. Dirt caked much of its face. The nose and eye sockets were empty, their contents, presumably, having been eaten by insects some time ago.

The corpse's jaw lowered, and it uttered a guttural sound that was close to "Come!"

The eye, which had been hovering safely near the tombstone, suddenly picked up momentum, spun around and lodged itself into one of the corpse's empty eye sockets. It rolled around inside the socket like it was in a slot machine, finally coming to rest with the pupil pointed out at the world. The corpse blinked a flap of putrefying flesh over Jane's eye. She could still see out of it.

The corpse took a look at the world around it, stopping when it came to gaze upon Jane. "A pleasure, miss," it said with a nod and a wink. It smiled a creepy smile. A few centipedes slipped through the gaps between its teeth.

Jane swallowed her fear and regarded the corpse. It would not do to start screaming and throwing a fit. Jane wanted her eye back, and she was going to have it. "I know what you're looking at, Mr. Crumb," she told it.

"Do you, now?"

"You're staring at my eye."

"**With** your eye, I might add." The corpse struggled to inch itself out of the hole in the ground. "Two eyes gives one... *depth perception*." The corpse dug its hands into the earth and tried to heave its upper body farther out. It looked like hard work, this rising-from-the-grave business. The corpse panted for breath. Jane wondered for a moment how that was even possible. Presumably, its lungs had long since disintegrated. Then the corpse extended a withered arm for Jane. "Can you give me a hand?"

Jane took a step back, and the corpse let out a stomach-churning chuckle. "I kill myself," the corpse gurgled. "Never mind, you go and run. I have one of your eyes now, so I can see what you see—"

"Get somebody else's eye!" Jane screamed.

The corpse shook its head. "Would you slip your feet into a pair of mismatched socks? Of course not. These things need to be matched perfectly."

Jane looked away. Then she saw something that gave her an idea. It was the nearby tree. The tree was beyond dead, a mummified shell. The roots stuck out of the ground. The blowing wind was causing the whole trunk to rock back and forth.

The tree was angled toward the tombstone. Jane remembered how soft and fragile the tombstone had been when she had gone to do her rubbing. All it needed was one solid push...a push from a tree...and the tombstone would fall like dominoes.

Like the books perched above Matteo's bed.

The corpse's head was still directly under the tombstone. Jane ran.

"That's right, you get a good head start," the corpse yelled as Jane left its field of vision. "But there's nothing in this world that can stop me from—"

The corpse did not hear the snapping of branches and roots. Nor did it hear the crackle of timber as the tree toppled into the tombstone. And it certainly didn't hear the stone crack in two. The stone landed squarely on the back of the corpse's exposed skull, and then it was buried beneath the dirt once again.

Jane shut her eye and tried to concentrate on what the other eye was seeing, but all her mind broadcast was blackness.

But then there was something else—something wriggling in front of her pupil. Jane concentrated hard, trying desperately to focus on what the other eye was seeing.

Correction. It was wriggling **things**. Jane could see them up close, as if she were looking through a microscope. She had seen the nature documentaries—she knew a nest of hungry ants when she saw it.

"**Bon appétit**," she said with a sigh. Then she turned around and trudged home. Her optometrist was going to have a field day with this one...

"So what seems to be the problem, Matteo?"

"My eye."

"What about it?"

"It *hurts*." Matteo couldn't explain anything beyond a word or two. Both of his eyes were overflowing with hot tears. They could have been acid for all Matteo knew—he had never known such pain.

"Can you open it up for me?"

Matteo shook his head. The doctor smiled. "I might give you a lollipop if you do." But Matteo wasn't buying into that garbage.

The doctor shrugged. "How did you hurt it then?"

"Paper cut."

"A *paper cut*?"

His eyes still shut, Matteo handed the piece of paper to the doctor. It was a rubbing, the doctor noted, most likely from a tombstone. What else would read *HERE LIES SHAWN CRUMB*?

THE PAGE TURNER

On the first Friday of every month, Mrs. Morley handed out the book-club catalogs that came from some huge publisher.

Anika's parents weren't big fans of the book club. *It's just an excuse for us to spend more money,* they would say. *There are plenty of books in the library.*

Still, all the other kids in her class ordered books from the monthly catalog. Why shouldn't she? Maybe she could pick one of the cheaper books.

As the rest of the class gathered together in small groups and pored over their catalogs, Anika, who had always been a good reader, narrowed her eyes. She was good at spotting details, like whenever a textbook had a spelling mistake.

The back of the catalog always had an itemized list of all the books and their prices. Anika usually looked at it only if she was going to order something, but today she was bored. She turned the catalog over and studied the long list of numbers.

Then she blinked.

For some reason a title right near the bottom of the list jumped out at her. It was called *Your Biography*, and it was listed at a completely reasonable $2.99.

Anika narrowed her eyes. What did that even mean, *Your Biography*? Whose biography? A biography was the story of somebody's life, so you'd think they would mention the subject of the book. It was obviously some kind of gimmick. Maybe it was just a blank notebook that you could use as a scrapbook to write your own life story.

She flipped back to the rest of the catalog and scanned the pictures and descriptions of the books.

There was no mention anywhere else of any biography.

She turned back to the order form at the end. She hadn't imagined it. *Your Biography* for $2.99.

Why sell something that wasn't even advertised? Even though she was sure the book would probably be boring, or a weird joke, Anika was curious. For three dollars she could have her answer.

Two weeks later it arrived. "Anika Singh," said Mrs. Morley, a slim volume pinched between her thumb and index finger.

The cover was red with bold letters in yellow: **YOUR BIOGRAPHY**.

There was no image and no author name.

Anika turned the book over to see if there was any information on the back cover. It was red like the front but with no words or markings.

Anika looked around to see what kind of books the other kids had ordered. Clusters of students were gathering around the desks of those who had received theirs. There were books about zombies and sharks, books about superheroes, books of world records and books about superhero zombie sharks.

Nobody had come to visit Anika's desk, and that suited her fine.

She opened the book and started to thumb through the pages. There were words printed on them, but as she scanned the volume, she encountered a clump of pages that were stuck together.

Anika tried pulling them apart with her fingers, but the pages would not yield to the pressure.

She frowned. Why couldn't she flip through all the pages? Had something been spilled on the book, making the pages stick together? Or was this some weird misprint? She wanted to ask Mrs. Morley, but the teacher was busy breaking up a fight two boys were having over the zombie book.

Anika sighed and decided to explore the matter herself.

She opened up the book again and started to go through the contents more carefully.

Most books had a page at the beginning listing publication information—author, publisher and some indication of when and where it was printed.

Not *Your Biography*.
The first page had the title.
Anika turned the page.

Dear Reader,

In your hands you are holding a most unique book. This is Your Biography, *created especially for you.*

This book is a living, working document. It is a professionally written biography of your own life.

You are probably wondering how such a feat can be achieved. How is it that we, the publisher, know your life story?

That is our little secret. While you may not get to know how the publishing miracle you are reading came to be, we are certain that you will enjoy it. Just turn the page and you will encounter a thoroughly detailed narrative of your own life, commencing with your birth and, of course, ending with your death.

No doubt you are asking how a mere book can know anything beyond the present moment. How can it know what the outcome of your future will be? What you will do after school? What you will do for a living? Will you get married? Are there children in your future? Most important, how could a book possibly know the date and means of your own death?

This book is, as we have already stated, a living document. It will write itself as you continue to live and grow.

Please note: it is important that you do not attempt to correlate the physical size of the book with the length of your own life.

The pages beyond the present moment have not been written yet, and many have been bonded together until the time they are ready to be read. They will be as thin or thick as they need to be, depending on the choices you make and the direction your life takes you.

It is very important that you do not attempt to separate the unwritten pages. We have gone to great lengths to ensure that they are not tampered with.

It could be very dangerous to interfere with the way Your Biography *is meant to be read.*

With that being said, please enjoy this most unique of books. It is not made available to everyone. You must be truly special and unique to have found it at all. Treat these pages well, and you will be rewarded with a memoir of your life to treasure for generations to come.

Sincerely,

The Publisher

Anika looked up and narrowed her eyes. This was clearly some kind of joke book, and the joke was on her.

A biography of her own life that wrote itself? Ridiculous.

Nevertheless, how good was the joke? She looked back down at the book and turned to the next page.

Anika Singh was born at the Dundurn County Hospital on a stormy Sunday afternoon after twenty-three grueling hours of labor.

Anika gasped. It was one thing to have a biography that had been preprinted and that had even slotted in her name.

She'd ordered the book herself, so it wouldn't have been hard for the publisher to digitally insert her name into the book in predetermined places and print it on demand.

But the details! Anika knew exactly how long her mother had been in labor. She talked about it all the time. And the hospital and city in which Anika had been born were accurate. But those details were not common knowledge. How could they be in the book?

Anika thumbed through the pages and took a closer look at some of the passages. There were many specific details she remembered from her life. One paragraph outlined a trip she took to the amusement park when she was five, and she ate too much waffle cake and got sick on one of the rides. Flipping forward, she encountered the story of her trip to the hospital when she broke her arm.

The details in the book were so crisp and clear that they reawakened memories she thought she'd lost.

Reading the biography was like opening a window into those memories. Whenever she wanted to, she could turn to a chapter in her own life and re-experience it as if for the first time.

Anika wondered how far the biography went.

She skipped to the back of the book.

Anika stared at the book and was incredulous. How could such a thing actually exist?

She flipped through the book and discovered that some pages were fused together, while others contained text.

Thinking the book was some kind of joke, Anika returned to the first page and read a passage outlining her birth. It contained details that only Anika and her family could know.

She wondered how the author of the biography, or even the book publisher, might have accessed such information.

She began to grow suspicious.

Anika lowered the book and stared around the room. She wondered if someone was watching her, making notes, somehow, and updating the book.

Maybe Mrs. Morley was in on the whole thing. She was the one who'd given out the book-club forms in the first place. Maybe she had some sort of weird deal with the publisher. It didn't all add up, but what other explanation was there?

Anika looked back down at the book.

One of the pages had come loose from the clump that had been stuck together. She turned the page and was amazed to discover that new text had been added.

Anika lowered her book and stared around the room. She wondered if someone was watching her, making notes, somehow, and updating the book.

Anika gasped and swallowed. The biography had caught up with her real life!

Anika noticed that one of the pages had come loose from the clump. She turned the page and was amazed to discover that new text had been added.

Anika gasped and swallowed. The biography had caught up with her real life!

She stared at the words and noticed how they mimicked her own thoughts. A weird sort of déjà vu crept over her.

Usually such a feeling only lasted for a moment, but as Anika read the biography, that feeling of having lived this moment grew more and more intense with each passing sentence. What she was reading was happening to her at that very moment. She wondered what might happen if she looked away from the book, got up from her seat and went to sharpen her pencil. When she returned, would the book have documented it?

As she wondered this, she noticed that the words in the book were following her train of thought. Anika shivered. Was it really her own train of thought, or was she was just thinking what the book was making her think?

The more she tried to wrap her brain around the enigmatic nature of the biography, the quicker she felt her heartbeat race, the sweatier her palms grew and the shorter each breath became. She was growing fearful. She decided to close the book and sharpen that pencil after all.

Anika slammed the book shut.

She took several long, deep breaths.

"Is everything all right, Anika?" Mrs. Morley asked.

Anika looked up. She could feel her body shaking and trembling.

Mrs. Morley was the only one who could possibly have anything to do with this. She was only pretending to look concerned. She knew Anika must be freaking out over the book.

Anika wasn't going to give Mrs. Morley the satisfaction. "I...need to sharpen my pencil, that's all."

Mrs. Morley stared at her. "Anika, are you sure you're all right?"

"Mmm-hmm."

Shakily Anika got up from her desk, edged over to the electric sharpener and chiseled the end of her pencil to a fine point.

She returned to her desk and sat down in front of the book.

She took a few deep breaths, thinking about her next move.

Then she opened the book. Sure enough, the words on the latest page read:

Back from sharpening her pencil, Anika thought about her next move.

She wasn't sure if the book knew what she was planning, but Anika was determined to unravel the mysteries of **Your Biography.**

She jammed the tip of the pencil into the thick clump of papers at the end of the book and worked at prying part of one page loose. Would the book yield a glimpse into her future?

The book did not want to yield. Anika was convinced it was literally clinging to the page, trying desperately to hold on to its secrets. But this time Anika had the upper hand. Literally.

With a swift yank, Anika wedged a page open.

"Aha!"

There was nothing there. No words, no text. Just a blank page.

So the book **couldn't** tell her future after all.

Anika gave a slight, satisfied smile and looked up. A few of her classmates were looking in her direction, probably curious about why she had cried out, but they soon went back to what they were doing. Anika was alone again.

She looked back down at the blank page, and—

The page wasn't blank anymore.

Anika, please stop.

No. It wasn't possible. Anika tried to blink the words off the page, but they had appeared and would not vanish.

She would not let this book get the better of her. She jammed her pencil between another clump of pages, pried them apart and stared at the empty white surface before her.

She nodded, feeling victorious.

She blinked, and more words appeared across the page.

You don't understand what will happen. The book cannot tell your future.

"No," Anika said out loud. She honestly didn't care if the book tried to tell her future or not. She wanted to know how it worked and why it was doing this to her. Again she pulled open a new spread.

Expecting to find a blank page, she was surprised to read a brief message, hastily scrawled in handwriting.

You are using up the pages!

Heart in her throat, Anika dug her fingernails deep into the last chunk of the book's bound pages. She could feel the book resist—like a clam or a mussel holding on to its own flesh for dear life—but she was stronger and more determined.

She forced the pages open. She was nearly at the last one.

This time the writing was smeared across the page in dark, inky blotches:

When you run out of pages, you run out of...

Anika gasped and turned the page over, then realized she had reached the very last page.

The book fell from her hands.

Anika screamed, but it wasn't a long scream.

She'd run out.

YOUR BIOGRAPHY

Dear Reader,

In your hands you are holding a most unique book. This is Your Biography, *created especially for you.*

This book is a living, working document. It is a professionally written biography of your own life.

You are probably wondering how such a feat can be achieved. How is it that we, the publisher, know your life story?

That is our little secret. While you may not get to know how the publishing miracle you are reading came to be, we are certain that you will enjoy it. Just turn the page and you will encounter a thoroughly detailed narrative of your own life, commencing with your birth and, of course, ending with your death.

No doubt you are asking how a mere book can know anything beyond the present moment. How can it know what the outcome of your future will be? What you will do after school? What you will do for a living? Will you get married? Are there children in your future? Most important, how could a book possibly know the date and means of your own death?

This book is, as we have already stated, a living document. It will write itself as you continue to live and grow.

Please note: it is important that you do not attempt to correlate the physical size of the book with the length of your own life.

The pages beyond the present moment have not been written yet, and many have been bonded together until the time they are ready to be read. They will be as thin or thick as they need to be, depending on the choices you make and the direction your life takes you.

It is very important that you do not attempt to separate the unwritten pages. We have gone to great lengths to ensure that they are not tampered with.

It could be very dangerous to interfere with the way Your Biography *is meant to be read.*

With that being said, please enjoy this most unique of books. It is not made available to everyone. You must be truly special and unique to have found it at all. Treat these pages well, and you will be rewarded with a memoir of your life to treasure for generations to come.

Sincerely,

The Publisher

WARNING

Your biography is still being written into this book. The following pages should not be tampered with on any account. Do not flip ahead.

You don't understand what will happen.
The book cannot tell your future.

You are using up
the pages!

When you run out
of pages,
you run out of...